CO 2 39 78

CW01103006

Ⓐ

THE KILLER STAMP

They had plenty of reasons for hating his guts! The three hard-cases caught up with Jim Gallery and decided he would have to die a nasty death because he had tricked them. But a night in an old Indian well full of turbulent flood water did not put an end to Jim. And the three hell-bents did not have any luck with Colts, Winchesters and other hardware.

Death and gold played a part on trails through Colorado to the Yellow Stones and hatreds boiled up. And a girl called Helen had more influence on Gallery than all the wealth they dug out of the ground.

This fast-moving novel cannot easily be put down once the reader has started on the trail.

By the same author

**Lawless Hideout
Desert Trails
Hell-Bent Gents
Colt Flame**

THE KILLER STAMP

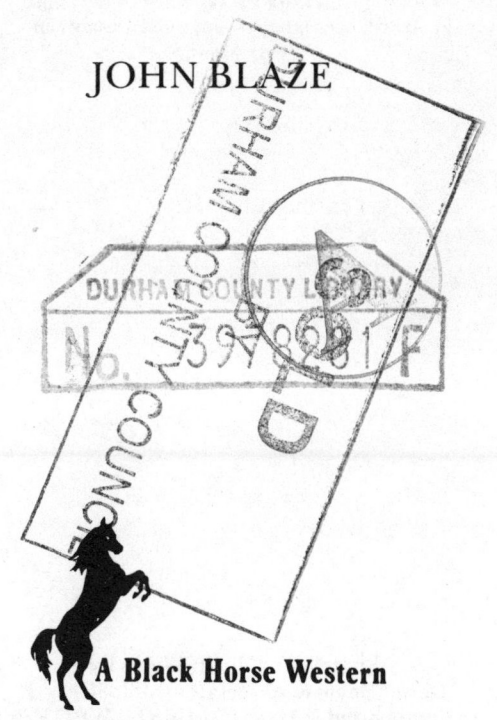

JOHN BLAZE

A Black Horse Western

ROBERT HALE · LONDON

© John Blaze 1991
First published in Great Britain 1991

ISBN 0 7090 4549 2

Robert Hale Limited
Clerkenwell House
Clerkenwell Green
London EC1R 0HT

The right of John Blaze to be identified as
author of this work has been asserted by him
in accordance with the Copyright, Designs and
Patents Act 1988.

Photoset in North Wales by
Derek Doyle & Associates, Mold, Clwyd.
Printed and bound in Great Britain by WBC Print Ltd,
and WBC Bookbinders Ltd, Bridgend, Mid Glamorgan.

One

Way up in the San Juan Mountains, some forty arid miles out of Delta, they were sure they had him cornered at last, and in the grimmest possible way. They had chased him right into this south-west corner of Colorado, avoiding towns where they might be known to a sheriff.

Jim Gallery had been bone-tired and weary when they had crept up on him. He thought he'd made no mistakes. He'd picked the rockiest way through the yellow canyons; he hadn't made a fire that night. Still, they'd crept up on him. The one mistake he had made was to get too tired.

Head on the ground, with only a blanket between him and the sand, his fatigued brain had heard the sound of scuffling boots a few dazed seconds too late. And then they had been on him. Three of the hardest ruffians unhanged this side of hell. A boot in his ribs had been the first notification of grief. They stood over him – tall, lean, unshaven, dirty hombres packing six-guns that looked like small cannons. They had plenty of reasons for hating his guts.

Blue-eyed blubbery-faced Kid Dawson hated him because he had killed his brother – in a fair fight, most men had agreed.

Max Kerle hated him because of money — the loot from the Drago Cattlemen's Bank, which had unaccountably been lost and stayed lost according to Jim Gallery. Max Kerle was a gangling, hawklike man who was wanted for robbery and murder right through Colorado and Wyoming.

And lastly, Stephen Crane, the older man, six feet of hard bone and stringy flesh, the man who still retained a cultured English accent along with an inhuman pleasure in cruelty of any kind. Flecks of grey in his hair and moustache gave him some dignity — but it was a disguise, for his soul was evil.

Jim Gallery rolled between their dusty boots as they kicked out in instant revenge for the arduous ride he had forced on them. He jerked like a creature seeking escape from a natural predator. He knew damned well there wasn't any escape but he reacted like a coiled spring to the kicks, trying to avoid them. But they landed. A boot in his gut sickened him; another to the head dazed him, and a kick in the ribs went like a knife-wound through his tired body. All the time, in spite of being dazed and in pain, he tried to jerk away.

They had taken his gun a moment before alarm bells went off in his head, so there was no hope of a shoot-out. His horse and rifle were some distance away, stashed in a rocky cleft.

They kicked at him until blood spurted in a red torrent from his nose and face. They kicked until his ribs ached. Twice they hit him in the crotch and he felt his senses swimming into a lousy world of sheer pain. He sprawled, unable even to jerk like some impaled creature, almost out of conscious senses, with only his unbeatable sense of survival keeping him aware of things. He had one thought;

The Killer Stamp

he would fight until he died. He was pretty sure now he would die – right here in this goddam arid land.

He had ridden into the badlands with the express purpose of losing his pursuers. He would have much preferred to have stayed in Delta – or Salida – drinking and complimenting the women, but he had to ride out when he heard that Kid Dawson, Max Kerle and Stephen Crane were on his trail. He'd ridden out only a day ahead of the unholy trio. Seemed it had been a lot of hard riding for nothing.

'We don't want to kill – not yet, my friends – perhaps we can think of a slower death for him than the merciful bullet!'

'He gun-marched you to the blamed sheriff in Alamosa – for the bounty, Crane!' Kid Dawson blazed. 'You hate his guts for that …'

'It was a neat trick I won't forget,' admitted Stephen Crane. 'But that jail couldn't hold me. I was in worse holes in India, many years ago.'

'When you was an officer and a gent in the goddam English army,' sneered Max Kerle. 'Yeah, we heard about it – you done told us plenty of times.'

'British army, you lanky ruffian,' corrected Stephen Crane with a sneer.

'And you got chucked out!' went on Max Kerle. 'You ain't so clever at explainin' just how come that happened. But what the hell! What now? We got Gallery – do we kill him or not?'

Kid Dawson looked up at the darkening sky. A moon began to show behind some clouds and there was a rising wind. 'I figure there's a storm blowing up – an' them blamed horses are tuckered out. We could kill him – get rid of him – and then we might be set for the night.'

'You lack finesse, young man,' said Stephen Crane. 'This devil killed your brother and all you can conjure up in the way of revenge is a fast slug. Oh, no – he lives – at least until tomorrow – in some suspense – and then he should die in agony. Now in India, they have many exquisite ways of destroying a man.'

'Sure – we got Injuns here who can cook up the tortures of the damned,' snapped Max Kerle. 'But we ain't taking a week over killin' this skunk. I want out of this blasted territory.'

'Are you sure he really doesn't know where the money from the Drago bank is stashed?' asked Stephen Crane.

'There was me, Gallery and Al Aston on that bank job,' said Max Kerle. 'Aston had to ride out like all hell with the *dinero*, while me and Gallery fooled the possemen with false trails. We kicked up some miles between us along that Laramie range – in and out of them damned hills which we knew like the backs of our hands. Then we hightailed it to meet Aston with some new horses we'd bought – didn't want to steal horseflesh – that could've brought more law after us. When we finally hit the place where we had figured to find Aston –'

'He was there – dead!' supplied Stephen Crane impatiently. 'Yes, you've told us this tale many times. He was dead and the bank loot was nowhere in sight. You and Gallery searched for hiding-places – looked for tracks of the killer –'

'Hoofmarks leading to the river,' grunted Max Kerle. 'The skunk must've ridden up and down the river for miles. We never cut sign of him again. A real smart hombre – whoever he was!'

Stephen Crane smiled and revealed teeth which were perfectly white, unusual for a man of his age in this frontier world. 'But you got around to thinking that somehow Gallery had pulled this trick. Because only you and Gallery knew that Al Aston would be hiding up in the hills near the river. Gallery could have had an accomplice.'

Max Kerle glared down at Jim Gallery as he rested warily on the ground, ready to jerk into action if he got half a chance – or to twist to avoid another kick. Blood smeared his face, making it a mask. He made gurgling sounds in his nose and throat as he attempted to breathe properly. He knew already bruises were forming on his body.

'He said it was some blasted stranger that robbed Al Aston,' snarled Max Kerle. 'I dunno ... maybe ...'

'Gallery never spent the money – that we do know. He didn't live high, wide and handsome like some men might have done. I think, my lanky *segundo*, that there is some element of doubt ...'

'All that damned *dinero!*' The other man went into one of his quick rages. 'Twenty thousand dollars – biggest thing I ever pulled – or any hold-up gent could ever hope to pull!'

'You, Gallery and the late unlamented Al Aston,' corrected the other man. 'You didn't perform the trick all alone. Yes, a neat little mystery which I admit intrigues me.' He looked down thoughtfully at the man crouching at their feet. 'You could try persuading Gallery to tell the truth now, Kerle.'

The gangling, hawk-faced man looked at the prisoner with some deep bitterness mixed with grudging respect. 'He'd never tell me anythin' but the tale as it stands.'

Kid Dawson glanced at the dark sky once more. 'Sure is a storm comin' up. I reckon we should find some place to shelter. I figure it will rain. I've seen these signs afore.'

'Ain't had rain for two months,' said Max Kerle.

'Wal, when it rains in this territory, it sure makes a helluva splash. I've seen these electrical storms before.'

'Aw, there's a wind. Could blow miles away. Sure, it could rain, maybe twenty miles back in the mountains.'

'Tell him, Steve,' shrilled the younger man. 'Tell him we need some place to shelter.'

The greying head jerked angrily. 'I've told you to call me Crane! I'm not Steve to you! Damn you! I was never Steve to anyone. Some years ago you would have called me "Sir". And damned well stood to attention while you spoke!'

'Now ain't that mighty fine!' Max Kerle laughed coarsely and watched Kid Dawson and Stephen Crane with enjoyment. He always liked these exchanges, where the older man tried to exercise some authority, because, inwardly, he hated Crane's guts. If the man had dropped down dead, he'd have laughed and turned him over with a boot. Crane meant nothing to him. He was a riding partner and crooked, which meant he knew some tricks for making quick money.

'Oh – all right – Crane,' Kid Dawson slurred the reply. 'You get real mean at times – Crane –'

'Call him "Sir",' jeered Max Kerle. 'An' maybe you should learn to salute, huh!'

'I ain't never been in no army,' growled Kid Dawson. He stood with his legs apart, the stance of a gunny, with his hands habitually at hip height. At one time, full of arrogance, Kid Dawson had packed twin Colts, until he realized they attracted unwelcome attention from other gun-happy characters, and he still had the habit of reaching for two guns. His blue eyes and curly hair had earned him the title of 'Kid' although he was about twenty-four. Now, dusty and smelling odorously of horseflesh and human sweat, he looked like the others, range-weary hombres who needed rest.

'I just figure we need some place to camp the night,' he moaned.

Stephen Crane could always infuse cold authority into his even voice. 'Perhaps you're right, Dawson. It may rain. Well, I noticed a cave on the way up to this spot. We'll go there – and take our prisoner with us for further punishment.'

Max Kerle grinned sardonically, rubbing a hard, long-fingered hand over the week-old stubble on his chin. Kid Dawson nodded, his fleshy round face satisfied. The men turned for their horses, and at that moment Jim Gallery uncoiled with the speed of a scared antelope.

He had figured a split-second chance was better than none at all. A man could get lost in the surrounding darkness in no time – if he was lucky.

But Max Kerle had reactions to match his hawklike features and he dived in the same second that Jim Gallery struck for freedom. The two men collided. The thud could be heard distinctly.

And then they were fighting, one man with desperate urgency and the other with vicious enjoyment. Jim Gallery stood little chance because of the punishment he had already taken, and Max Kerle knew that. He was able to sink a right and left fist into a weakened man. He felt Jim Gallery sag.

He hit him again, a body blow, as if his opponent was a punch-bag. Jim Gallery rolled back to the earth, gasping.

'Hell, you ain't so tough, Gallery!' A sneering laugh. 'Figured you were rock at one time. Maybe you've gone soft!'

'Put a loop around his neck,' ordered Stephen Crane. 'Let's get to saddle – and find his horse. We'll ride down to that cave. I must confess I suddenly feel the need for food and rest.'

A sneer curved the whiskered lips of Max Kerle but he made no reply. One thing he knew for sure; he was mighty tired of the other man's fancy talk. He figured he didn't like Englishmen; a ranny in these western lands should use the real lingo. Well, they'd found Gallery and maybe that would be the end of riding with Stephen Crane – unless there was some money to be made. In which case he might go along with the sneering galoot.

The cave was large and dry and they could hear running water not far away. At the moment their canteens held sufficient. Still, the cave seemed a good spot. There was a grassy little nook which would shelter the horses for the night. Flat slabs of rock, weathered by unknown years of wind, rain and sandstorm lay in front of the cave. In the faint light from the cloud-obscured moon, Stephen Crane found a curious hole in the rocky ground about a hundred yards from the cave mouth. It was almost like a well – a shaft. It had smooth sides and was about two yards in diameter and seemingly went down for about twenty feet.

He studied it for some moments and a cruel smile twisted his moustached lip. He went back to the others and surveyed Jim Gallery.

The Killer Stamp

'I've found a neat little cell for you, my man. Not an iron bar in sight – but better than that insalubrious hole into which you had me marched! Better because you will be unable to climb out. Even a lizard couldn't get out of that well.'

He was so enthusiastic about his find that he got the other two men to push Jim Gallery along to the smooth, round, rocky hole in the ground. They looked down and agreed that even a sidewinder could not climb out of that well. Then they grabbed Jim Gallery, shoved him to the edge of the hole and dropped him into the smooth circular shaft.

Jim hit the bottom of the well with a thud that made his guts jerk. He lay dazed. When he stirred again his first thought was that no bones had been broken. He could move without agony. Still, he suffered physically. He had been knocked around by vicious men and now he had been dropped some distance into this well. He was bruised and hurt. His pants were torn and skin was scraped from his knees. Blood thickened on his face, clinging to his beard stubble. He was in bad shape.

He sat up, scowling fiercely and looked around. Then, slowly, he got to his feet and moved around, hands splaying over the smooth walls of the well. It was a curious place, part natural and part man-made, he figured. Maybe some cave-dwellers long ago had fashioned the well. These thoughts did not matter a damn now. How could he get out? Or was he trapped?

He tried bracing himself against the wall and ramming his boots on the other side, but even with his six feet of length it was hard to get much leverage. He tried it, with his hands hard against one side of the smooth perimeter and his feet braced hard against the other side. It was a muscle-wracking effort that got him about six feet from the bottom of the well and then he could not maintain the strain any longer. He dropped back, boots scuffing the loose chippings at the bottom of the well.

Well, he had been outsmarted! They'd got him! Three men with good reason to hate his guts! Max Kerle and his reaction to the missing loot; Kid Dawson who kept his resentment about his dead brother – whom no man had ever missed – as if it was a religion; and Stephen Crane, who felt evilly disposed to a man who had attempted to use him for bounty money. Sure, they all had good cause to hate him.

Jim Gallery stared at the distant circle of sky above his head and in the faint light of the night saw the blacker clouds move ominously across the sky. Kid Dawson was right about the oncoming storm but maybe it would be highly localized and miss this area.

He glared again at the round patch of sky. He picked up a stone and tried to gouge a foothold in the wall of the well. The stone was too soft and he threw it away in disgust. He searched around for something harder but there was nothing. They had taken his gun and knife, naturally. So he had nothing except his fingernails. Anyway, it was an impossible task. And if they allowed him to live – or die – in this well, the sun would bake him into exhaustion and death in no time.

Maybe this was it, the end of the trail for one Jim Gallery. Well, he'd had a good time, not all of it morally creditworthy, he supposed. He'd been a bad 'un at times – but maybe not all bad. He had tried to do some good things along the way. He had helped with a wagon train; nursed another man to health; even helped Indian women and kids. And there had been Molly Peterson. She had been the one person he should have stayed with, but the old wanderlust had beckoned. Molly! Lovely Molly! Maybe she was still in Denver, looking back at the shadow of the mountains and wondering if he would ride back one day. Maybe! Maybe she had got herself a new man and married.

Jim Gallery sat down, crouched, his head between his knees, nursing his aches and pains, his mind full of many regretful things.

In the nearby cave the three hard-cases stretched out, blankets under them, and stared at the fire in the cave mouth. They had the pleasure of hot coffee and a cooked slab of sidemeat from which they sliced chunks. They had hardtack and some three-day-old buns.

And then they suddenly heard the storm break. A flash of lightning cut the night sky and thunder rolled. The rain came a moment later, a slashing deluge that spat at the parched earth as if in a frenzy.

Two

They listened to the pouring rain for a long time, noting the many flashes of blue lightning, secure in the cave, the fire just out of reach of the water and now a comforting mass of red embers. Kid Dawson kept on saying: 'Sure, I was right – real old downpour! Knew it would hit this area.'

'You don't know nothin'!' sneered Max Kerle. 'You're just making with the mouth, boy. Now shuddup!'

'That hellion out there will get mighty wet,' Kid Dawson gloated. 'Real cold and wet.'

'That's just too bad for him.'

'I hope he gets the shakes,' grated Stephen Crane. 'I'm not going out in this damned mess just to watch him – although it would be enjoyable to watch him gasping in that well.'

'Maybe he'll drown.'

'You lack logic, my friend,' sneered the other. 'Possibly the well will accumulate about three feet of water but that's all. Enough to give him a real wet night. And it will be cold out there.'

'The hell with him.'

Stephen Crane chuckled. 'That and the hiding we gave him will make Jim Gallery rather ill. But he'll die – tomorrow.'

'Who is gonna shoot him?' Kid Dawson looked eager. 'I'd like to fill him with lead – the slow way. Look what he did to my brother.'

'Filled him with lead, too,' retorted Max Kerle, laughing nastily. That quip was his idea of a joke.

'You can quit making out that that's funny,' growled Kid Dawson. 'Yeah – you kinda like to get at me, don'tcha?'

'Wal, you rise to the bait every time.'

'Haven't you two any better brand of conversation?' snarled Stephen Crane. 'God, it's like having to listen to morons continuously.'

A surly silence fell over the three men. The water pelted down outside, making rivulets that sought outlets on lower levels of the rocky terrain. The sound of the sluicing went on and on.

'Sure hope them hosses are all right.' Kid Dawson stirred the fire.

'They've got plenty of cover in that nook.'

'Sure would like to see that bastard gaspin' in that well.'

'Why don't you go an' take a looksee?' sneered Max Kerle. 'You'd get a wash into the bargain. Sure would do you a power of good – get rid of them desert fleas you got!'

'Why – you – you –' Kid Dawson jerked into a threatening stance, partly flinging his blanket to one side.

Stephen Crane said in sneering, bored tones: 'You two are like childish idiots. No discipline! God, what I've come down to! Now in my regiment …'

'The hell with your blamed regiment!' Max Kerle flung the retort like a challenge. Eyes clashed. Pure antagonism flared across the cave while the storm raged on outside.

Stephen Crane enjoyed pouring out venom; there was a need in him to make himself feel superior. 'We are undoubtedly not the most congenial company for each other.' His voice changed. 'I think after tonight we had better split up. We've accomplished our purpose. Gallery will be dead. I think we'd better ride separate ways. Too bad, Kerle, my man, you failed to locate the missing Drago money.'

'Gallery sticks to his tale – Al Aston was robbed.'

The other man nodded. 'Could be true. You watched Gallery for months after the robbery. You say he never spent a cent above his average earnings. To a man like Gallery, fond of the ladies and a night or two at the gaming tables, to have money close to hand and be unable to spend it would be almost intolerable.'

'I watched him in Laramie and Boulder,' said Kerle. 'He didn't know I was around, I can tell you. I followed him at times. He never spent any real *dinero* all that time. If I'd thought he had it stashed away, I'd ha' been on to him.'

Stephen Crane nodded. 'Regrettable that this mystery will haunt you for the rest of your miserable days – because Gallery will die tomorrow.'

They had eaten and it was natural to feel drowsy because they had endured a hard day in the saddle. They were well wrapped up and warm air circled back into the cave from the fire. Their personal animosites could not be maintained and so they fell asleep. The rain outside slashed down and scoured another layer of yellow dust from the bedrock all around the site. The water gurgled energetically along a thousand crevices, down across the slabs of rock, and along to the ancient well. The hole had been constructed in the ancient past for that very purpose.

Jim Gallery stood chest-high in the muddy swirl and stared at the round patch of darkened sky which seemed just beyond his reach. He had yelled for help but there was no one to hear – or care. The thunder had ceased along with the wicked flashes of lightning but the rain continued to fall steadily, sheets of the stuff, and water poured into the well from a dozen different directions.

As he stared upwards, his dark hair lank and clinging, his face with its unmistakable Irish heritage became lined and grim. He was scared. The well was filling. At this rate it would be over his head eventually. How long would it rain? He was as cold as a two-day corpse but not quite as stiff. He felt gut-hungry – but there could be worse things than hunger ahead of him. He was also physically weak on account of the beatings he had taken.

Far from slackening off, the rain fell steadily, as if the floods of old had returned. The water in the well lapped to his chest – then to his chin and mouth. He knew it was time for him to relearn an art he had seldom practised since boyhood. He'd have to learn to swim again!

He flicked off his boots and then splashed out, remembering how to tread water. He sure wasn't going to swim anywhere. The water lapped to his chin and his mouth, the well filling steadily. Pretty soon he was churning around like some drowning cur in a hole in the ground. Water poured in from above in about four main spouts and he had to avoid these torrents. He found a side of the well that was relatively free of waterfalls. He stayed there and made a discovery.

The rising water had carried him up to a point where the side of the ancient well was a bit rough and this afforded him a precarious handgrip. He hung on, his feet churning like mad. He looked up to the edge of the well. It was still a long way off, beyond his utmost frantic reach. Would he drown when exhaustion overcame him?

Somewhere, miles away, the thunder rolled across the heavens again. The wind was rising steadily again, moaning like a vengeful devil. A freak wind blew harshly for some time and brought the storm centre back over the hills. The rain as a consequence came down with renewed ferocity.

The men in the cave did not hear anything but deluging water. Maybe they were so tired that background noises meant nothing to them. They slept soundly. The wind and rain lashed into the age-old barriers of rock-cliff and bedrock. Finally before the sun even showed the first feeble rays, the storm faded entirely and the cloud moved on under a strong wind.

The old rock-girt well shimmered with yellow floor water.

The men in the cave stirred, instinctively knowing this was another day, even through the dregs of sleep in their minds. One by one they got up and moved around in silence, sour men at that time of morning.

Kid Dawson was the first to say: 'I'll go an' take a looksee at the blamed prisoner ...'

'I'll come with you,' murmured Stephen Crane. 'Habit of a lifetime, you know – rising early –'

'Hell, don't talk to me about your lousy regiment again!'

Stephen Crane looked around. 'The earth smells sweet and cool —'

'Won't stay that way,' grunted Max Kerle. 'It'll heat up like an oven in those canyons. Let's go look at that tricky hombre ...'

They walked out of the cave, across the beds of rock. Kerle and Dawson had shoulders hunched, hands rammed into pants pockets. Stephen Crane, as always, walked erect, his arms swinging. None of the men had a gunbelt or a weapon in hand.

'Sure hope that cuss ain't too cold an' wet to talk back,' sniggered Kid Dawson. 'Say, how are we goin' to kill him? Do we draw lots, huh?'

'A knife in the guts is a real slow way.' Max Kerle kicked at a stone. 'Hell, I still ain't sure about him an' that *dinero*.'

They tramped up to the well and looked down. Surprise hit three grim faces. Yellow water lay placid and impenetrable to the top of the well. Nothing stirred in the yellow depths.

'Wal, damn — he drowned!' yelled Kid Dawson, his blubbery face like a punch-ball.

'Yeah — he's at the bottom of the hole.' Max Kerle began to laugh sourly. 'Wal, so much for that rock-hard galoot, Jim Gallery! Drowned like a mangy polecat in a ditch!'

Stephen Crane stared, eyes glinting. 'A miserable death — not that I care — but don't be too sure, my friends. God, I didn't think so much water would collect in this well — and yet I should have known. The place has been fashioned to collect water from all points. Look at the weathered channels leading to it!'

Max Kerle whipped around, glared at the hills, the rocky ledges and the stunted scrub bushes.

'Now, look, Crane – is he dead or not? What the blazes do you mean about not being too sure? How could a man get out of there? All that water! He'd ha' drowned!'

'The human body has buoyancy, you fool. Can't you swim? I guess you can't. Now a man who could keep afloat …'

Stephen Crane whipped around and began striding back, intent on an idea that had hit him like a landslide.

The other two men followed him out of habit. They could see by the grim way he strode on that there was something on his mind. And as they approached the nook where the horses had been tethered for the night, Max Kerle was the first to catch on. 'By thunder – the damned animals!'

'That's right,' sneered the other man. 'You've cottoned on!'

'Hosses!' yelled Dawson and he began to run. 'Hell – you don't mean –'

There was no need for a rush of words because when they rounded the rocky cleft everything was all too obvious. The animals had gone.

'By Gawd – he got outa that hole!' Max Kerle practically screamed. 'Gone! With four damned cayuses!'

Stephen Crane turned to Kid Dawson as if the young man was some new rookie in the infantry. The contempt in his tone was enough to poison any man against him. 'If I remember correctly, Dawson, you left your mount saddled. You were too lazy to strip it. He'll be riding your animal for sure. The others will be driven miles away by now.'

'Damned cuss!'

'The one thing I can't be sure of is just how long

he's been away.'

'Long enough,' snarled Max Kerle. He glared up at the sun, which was already a hot orb in the sky. 'It's gonna be hot as all hell in this area – an' us fools on foot!'

'We've got guns. We –'

'We've got to find that tricky bastard afore we can line a gun on him! You gone loco, Kid? Ain't you got no brains at all?'

'It weren't my idea to stick that swine in a goddam hole!' yelled Kid Dawson. 'I wanted him dead. You should ha' let me salivate him!'

'Are you implying that I made a mess of things?' gritted Stephen Crane. 'Well, there was no way of knowing so much water would funnel into the well – but I can see it now. Some Indians of long ago fashioned that hole for that express purpose – to catch water quickly.'

'So he kept afloat,' growled Max Kerle. 'An' then climbed out when the water carried him up to the rim of the well. Gee, that goddam hard-case! The devil looks after Jim Gallery. But I'm gonna kill that robbing skunk some day!'

'Is that so?' Kid Dawson resented the other man. 'Yeah – you tell me how we're goin' to walk forty miles to Delta.'

'Men have trailed further than that –'

'In this heat? We'll be more than tuckered out –'

Stephen Crane whipped around to them. 'We've got to get started. We might be able to find the horses. Gallery might have driven them off after a few miles.'

'He won't,' sneered Max Kerle. 'He won't run them loose under ten miles – an' they'll stray. On foot, might take us two days to track them critturs.'

'You plan to take up residence here?'

'Real fancy talk!' The other man practically spat the words. 'And that damned accent! When the hell are you goin' to talk like us?'

'My style of speech shouldn't concern an uneducated drifter like you –' With that rapped comment, which was designed to push Max Kerle right back into his place, Stephen Crane walked back to the cave where they had left their gear.

Here were piled saddles – but they were useless. Still, they had water canteens and plenty of water outside, but out in the hard country natural water from the storm would quickly evaporate. They had guns and rifles and some food. But all they had for transportation were their legs and like all range waddies they disliked walking. And in the hot badlands between this area and Delta a man could become mighty weary, possibly lamed.

Three grim men made preparations to move on, but not before there was some debate about the wisdom of tramping on oven-hot land during the time the sun was at its highest.

'We could move at night – be a damn sight cooler,' said Max Kerle.

'We'd never see the horses if we delay another eight hours,' countered Stephen Crane.

'Ain't no guarantee we'll ever sight 'em …'

'I know. But at night we won't even see Gallery's tracks.'

'He'll head for Delta – where else?'

'There's Salida – not that far to the east.'

'Too damned far for three hombres on foot,' Max Kerle put in. 'You know every blasted mile counts.'

'Delta, then,' commented the ex-army man.

'He's got no guns – an' no grub,' Kid Dawson pointed out. 'He ain't got all the aces – damn him! What'll he do for water?'

'You left your rig on that hoss. Like a fool! And you had two water bottles slung on it, if I rightly recall. Need to say any more?'

'He can ride that animal to death and make it quickly to Delta – or can take it easy for two days,' added Stephen Crane.

'He'd ha' taken a horse in any case and rode it barebacked,' retaliated the young guy. 'Lack of a saddle wouldn't have stopped that bastard ...'

'Lack of water canteens might,' Max Kerle's retort, full of hate for his younger pal, came back like a slug spitting through thin air. 'What the hell! Let's light out! Of all the blasted luck! We should have killed that hellion last night.'

Three grim men began preparations to move on, full of grim dislike of each other, and the common cause of ill-gotten gains quickly fading from all possibility.

Three

Jim Gallery rode grimly and tiredly, sitting his saddle like a hunched-up old man. He was tired as all hell. He had struggled for his life all night, fighting to survive, swimming like a rat in a barrel. He had hauled himself out of the well, blessing the torrential rain that had threatened to drown him. He had made his escape. He had fought his surroundings and won.

Like many a man in a primitive world he had felt sure there was someone, somewhere, helping him, but he was unable to probe any deeper into this philosophy. So much for the day. All that mattered to a hard-case rider was the realization that he was alive and free.

He had crept silently to the horses, his stockinged feet making him as silent as an Indian on the prowl. Fearful lest the animals might snicker, he had held his breath while he led them away.

At a wise distance he got aboard his own horse, liking the saddle, which seemed to fit his rump. He was glad the other hell-bents had rounded up all the animals. A nice package, complete with water canteens and Kid Dawson's gear.

He stopped again at the nearest pan of water to

fill the canteens, and then, with a rope trailing to the other horses, he rode on, guided by the position of the watery sun, now rising in the morning. He rode for about three hours, time on his side, he thought, at a steady pace, and then he released the other nags with a wild shout because he figured they were slowing him. If the other guys and their pals found the horses after that interval and distance they would be lucky – but still too late. All in all, he reckoned he'd have a good day's headstart – and that was enough for him.

But as the sun rose and the heat began to be fierce, he had to resort more and more to the water canteens. The animal needed water – very important.

So he stopped occasionally, staring at the arid conditions and wondering when he would reach grass for the cayuse's sake. He was hungry. He had rummaged in Kid Dawson's saddle-bag and found some stale buns. He blessed the arrogant young hard-case. But the buns were not enough to ease the gnawing feeling that comes with a really empty gut. There was nothing in this land he could chew on. He could not even find a lizard. He was weary, his bruises beginning to ache like some dull torment. He had taken several beatings and the fight for life in the well had sapped his strength.

Grim and cursing the land, he allowed the cayuse to plod on at its own pace because this was the wisest course. His stockinged feet pressed against hot stirrups and he wished he had his boots, but they were water-logged at the bottom of the old well.

He had gotten away from death by the skin of his teeth, leaving behind three men who would vow renewed vengeance. They'd more than hate his guts now!

He rode all day and used a canteen of water, for himself and for the horse. The animal was warm and alive beneath him, part of him, part of his fight to stay alive and he felt affinity with the crittur.

Then he led the animal into some broken land that showed signs of greenery. He spotted some clumps of juniper, hanging with berries, and knew there was water close by. He found it. The land slanted into a deep little vee, and there was the spring, bubbling between rocks, a mystery in this silent empty land. With the rains of the previous night feeding the underground channels, the spring was running full, and there was grass, tender and fresh for the horse. Pity he, too, couldn't eat grass because there was nothing else and he possessed neither gun nor knife with which to kill anything that moved. Not that anything did.

He sat that evening, with the sun ready to sink fast, his feet in a pool, his face bathed. The cuts and bruises had reached their fully swollen state and his ribs still ached where he had been kicked.

He was hitching the horse for the night, contemplating a quick getaway long before sunup, when he heard the slow, distant clop-clop of hoofs. He crouched, his brain leaping through the possibilities; Crane and his cronies could not have caught up with him. There was only one horse slowly moving. So this was some lone rider.

He wasn't really prepared to see a girl mounted on a big black mare, but she came swiftly into view and their eyes locked, hers questioningly, warily. She noted his lack of hardware, his puffed features, his lack of boots. She was a girl of fast reactions. As for Jim Gallery, there was some relief. He even managed a smile – which hurt.

'Howdy, ma'am!'

'Who are you? What are you doing here?' There was some fear in her voice, which he supposed was natural.

She sat the sleek black horse with some control, sitting side-saddle. She wore a long black skirt and a white blouse. Her dark hair, gleaming like the raven's wing, was coiled carefully at the back of her head. She was tanned, with a lovely skin. He thought: long time since I saw a lady side-saddle! He smiled again.

'I'm Jim –' He paused. 'That's enough. I'm here because I need to rest – and this is the best spot I've encountered in the past twenty miles.'

'You've come across the badlands?'

'If you really want to know – yes. And you, miss? Why're you out ridin' at this time o' night? It'll be really dark with no darned moon in about twenty minutes.'

'I have to ride,' she burst out. Her coolness left her. 'I've got to get to Delta …'

'That's a long way.'

'I know. I have to find a doctor.' She flung him a fast, careful glance. 'You're not one of the gang …'

'What gang?'

'You're not one of the men who shot my father – no – I don't think so – you don't look –'

'I'm not one of any gang. I'm a bit of a loner. How bad is your father?'

'He is losing blood. The bullet hit a vein in his shoulder and I tried to stem the flow – but – but –'

'It's a long way to Delta. You shouldn't have left him – if he's alone –'

'I panicked. I was scared.'

'Are you living around here somewheres? So near the wastelands? Why in God's name?'

'What's it to you?' she snapped, suddenly afraid. Then in some confusion: 'I'm sorry – I didn't mean to be rude – but –'

Jim Gallery moved purposefully. 'Wal, we're wasting time – daylight time. How far away do you live?'

'Just about two miles from here.'

'Let's get going. If he's bleeding badly, time is important.'

'But he needs a doctor …'

'I've done plenty of doctorin'. Bullet wounds a speciality. Ain't so good with measles or childbirth – that really scares me! But slugs I've fixed plenty.' He vaulted stiffly to his saddle. 'And maybe you've got some grub at home?'

'We've got plenty – yes.'

'I'm so hungry I could chew on a dead packhorse. And maybe if you've got a pair of boots – maybe your pa's spare pair – if he's got feet as big as mine!'

'He's a big man.' She looked carefully at him again. 'You've been in some trouble, huh? You've been fighting.'

He wheeled his horse. The animal snorted, resentful, reluctant to leave the green grass. He nudged it hard in the ribs with his knees and, with the girl, they sped into the rapidly darkening night.

A thought hit his mind. 'This gang who shot your Pa – how many galoots? And why? Why'd they shoot him?'

Her voice carried back through the cooler night air. 'I'll tell you later –'

The Killer Stamp

'When you've figured me out, huh?' Jim Gallery grinned. 'All right. It's a deal. Boots and grub – and I'll do my best for your pa. Then I'll ride on. Seems we're both lucky. You got a name, miss –'

'I'm Helen Mackay. My father is known to his few friends as Bert. We live alone.'

Jim Gallery nodded and got his mount moving smoothly. 'You know, that was a mighty dangerous trip you were contemplating. You – alone – at night – with twenty miles or so to Delta. Your pa could bleed to death long afore you got back. And what about this gang? Will they make a return visit?'

'I wasn't thinking properly. I said I'd tell you more later.'

'I'm Jim Gallery – drifter, hard-case.' He was slightly mocking.

'Oh!' She became silent. The horses moved as swiftly as they dared on the dark trail. After they had traversed some distance, the girl swung her animal towards some rising hills which even in the sundown light he knew were covered in clumps of wild sage and prickly chaparral. After another half-mile they rode through a narrow track through rocky outcrops that stood up like sentinels. Jim wondered just why this girl and her father were living out here in this wild land.

'When did your pa get shot?'

'Only an hour ago,' she shouted back. 'At first I tried to stop the bleeding but I just couldn't do it – and then I got scared and thought I'd ride out for a doc. I should have realized it all takes a lot of time.'

As they rode he noted the jagged rocks that stood up like giant teeth in all directions. Wind and rain had scoured this area for thousands of years, leaving the hard rock and cutting gullies in the soft.

And then quite suddenly he spotted the shack in the gathering gloom. The structure was pretty ramshackle, made of logs, lengths of clapboard, a sod roof and a porch of sun-bleached, unpainted wood. He saw the stone chimney stack at one side, useful for cold winter nights, and a rough corral to the right of the place.

As he rode up and dismounted, he saw the huge heaps of chipped stone. There were five such piles, all to the right of the shack, near the rocky cliff that faced the house. He formed a few instant ideas but there wasn't time for a look around. He had to attend a wounded man.

He had a feeling that Helen Mackay would never have brought him or anyone like him to this place had it not been for her injured father. Suddenly he had the hunch that there were secrets.

And then, seconds later, he was inside the place and bending over the man lying on a bunk in a separate room. Jim saw a big man, all of six feet he guessed, broad-shouldered. He had white bushy hair and a beard of the same hue. He seemed old to be the girl's father. His wound was really giving him pain and he grimaced when he saw Jim Gallery.

'Who the heck is this, Helen?'

'He's going to help you, Pa.'

The man grunted, snarled with pain and writhed. 'All right – just get this damned slug out, mister – an' be on your way!'

Jim Gallery grinned thinly and began working. He unwrapped the bloodstained bandages, just strips of cloth which the frightened girl had used. He found a nasty wound. The slug had torn into a vein and Bert Mackay had lost a lot of blood.

The Killer Stamp

The next ten minutes were punctuated by moans from the man and a few rapped commands from Jim Gallery to the girl. She brought a sharp pointed knife, the steel finely honed and good for the rough surgery he had to perform. She also brought him iodine, some pads of cloth and more fresh strips for bandages. There was no whisky in the shack; nothing the man could take to dull the pain of the rough operation. He just had to get relief through issuing his harsh moans and yells as the steel dug deep. Helen held him down. Jim Gallery worked as quickly as he could and the slug was eventually extracted and then the pads and bandages applied. Bert Mackay was limp by that time and he lay back with closed eyes.

'He'll be all right. If the bleeding stops, and I figure it will, he'll be up and around inside three days – but he won't be able to use that arm for some time.' Jim sluiced his hands in a bucket of cold water. Helen handed him a coarse towel. 'Now what about the grub – not to mention the boots?'

'You're welcome.' She looked thoughtfully at him.

'That's all I need – unless you got a gun you don't want. And a bunk for the night. I'll be on my way at sun-up.'

There were other chores to do, such as a feed for his horse. He removed the saddle, giving the mount some freedom. Outside, he stared at the heaps of stone chips and other loose rocky debris but the night had become really gloomy and he hadn't time nor inclination to stare around. So, shrugging, he went indoors again. Helen had made him a bed on the living-room floor. There were only two other rooms and she used one as her bedroom.

A few minutes later she had cooked him some grub; bacon, beans, fried bread and apple pie. He shovelled the food into him and then paused over a mug of black coffee.

He grinned. 'Sorry! I was starving. I'm darned tired, too. I'll turn in if you don't mind.'

'You don't want to ask questions?'

'No more than you want to ask me.'

'Oh – all right – but you must be curious …'

'And you, too.'

Twenty minutes later he was sound asleep, like a man in oblivion. In the other room, Helen Mackay lay with eyes wide open. Who was this stranger? A man dirty, unshaven, his face showing signs of a recent beating! He was gunless, without boots, in these badlands. Jim Gallery! Was he just a drifter, a hard-case – or just another western man in a vast country. Well, he had helped her and showed no signs of being nasty. And she thought, when his bruises healed, he would be real good-looking.

Her father would be all right now. A good thing she had met Jim Gallery. But the robbery rankled. Her father would be difficult to live with for some time. He'd rage for a long time – and with good reason. Months of work for nothing! Just to enrich two no-good hellions who had appeared from nowhere and demanded the gold. And when her father had rightly resisted, they had shot him – not to kill but simply to make him talk.

And when her father had staggered back with blood pouring from his shoulder, she had told the mean-looking rannigans where to find the cache of gold. She had feared they intended to kill her pa, and no amount of gold could be worth that risk.

Some hours later Jim Gallery stirred when the

sun had been playing on him for some time through a window. He lay, looking around. His clothes lay in a heap — the worse-for-wear brown pants, the black shirt and leather vest. They'd been soaked and dried in the sun. Blood had congealed on them and sweat had permeated them during the day-time ride.

Somehow the thought of the cool, clear-faced Helen Mackay lying in the other room could not leave his mind. He knew she was a pretty young woman, attractive to any man. In a way, she reminded him of Molly Peterson — the same lithe figure and dark hair. Maybe Molly had married some other hombre by now. If she had any sense, she would!

He got up. He dressed, tried on the boots Helen had got for him. They fitted reasonably well. He ran a hand over his stubble. Maybe her father had a razor. It might be a good idea if he smartened up a bit. In town he could look a real dandy, given the right outfit. Well, when he hit Delta, there'd be some changes. He had some money in a bank there. He'd buy some gear, maybe trade in for a new horse, although it would be hard to better his present crittur. He'd need guns — by heck he'd need a rifle and a Colt! Then he'd go and look for Henry Carslake, the tricky swine!

This was a big country but the bastard was somewhere, and maybe not too far, with the *dinero* from the Drago Cattleman's Bank.

Yeah, the money that men had killed and lied for!

Four

The three men were mean and bitter by the end of the first day's march over the bad terrain. True, they had plenty of water and some grub in the saddle-bags they carried over their shoulders, but that was only a slight help as they stumbled along in their high-heeled riding boots. They were en route to Delta, sure enough, and they had seen the tracks of the four horses right up to the spot where Jim Gallery had dispersed three of them. They had wasted much time trying to spot the animals from some high ground, but to no avail.

'We'll camp,' stated Stephen Crane, his grey moustache and face powdered with fine dust. 'Right here. With our backs to those damned rocks. That was always a good practice in India ...'

'This is Colorado, pal,' sneered Max Kerle. 'And the Cheyenne are peaceful from right here to Bent's Fort – but if you go south you're in Apache country an' that's different.'

'I do not need your educational efforts, Kerle,' came the angry retort. 'I merely said we'd camp here.'

'That damned snake, Jim Gallery, is miles ahead of us,' moaned Kid Dawson. 'And tomorrow with his mount fresh he'll push right into Delta. If he's got money stashed away in that burg, he could take the stage to Denver – or anywhere – but I'll find him. I've got my brother to think about. I cain't have that skunk boasting …'

'Gallery killed him fair an' square. Take a tip from that, Kid.'

'Hell, I'm sick of you tryin' to rile me!' The young buckeroo glared at Kerle. His hand flashed down to his hip. He had only one gun – but he did not lift it. He just fingered the butt, oozing hatred of the other man.

'Simmer down, you two,' Stephen Crane rapped.

'Don't talk to me like I was dirt!' Kid Dawson whipped around again, glaring at the tall older man. 'I'm sick to hell of you, too!'

Max Kerle tried again. 'If you ever catch up with that Gallery hombre, don't lose your cool – because he'll bury you.'

'I'm beginning to wonder why we ever decided to hunt Gallery together,' said Stephen Crane. 'We haven't much in common.'

'You figured there was some chance of learning about the Drago money!' Max Kerle couldn't resist the dig. 'It wasn't all on account of how Gallery offended you by marching you in for that bounty.'

'How very perceptive.' The other man sat down, his back to a rock, and began to search his saddle-bag for some food. 'But you knew Gallery would die before telling secrets. Oh, the devil take this miserable conversation! I wish to God I was with my regiment. At least my brother officers behaved like gentlemen.'

'Yeah – right up to the time they drummed you out. Or were you kicked out?' Max Kerle laughed grittily. He sat down, placed his rifle near to him. 'I need shut-eye. The hell with you two!'

He did not see the disdain in Stephen Crane's eyes; he was lying back, relaxed. He thought he would find a new partner some day, a guy who could hell around and spoke the same lingo. But they would have to finish the job of filling Gallery with lead. Right now he was stuck with Crane and Dawson. Damn them both!

Kid Dawson walked around the cluster of rocks and peered into the night air. His hatred for Gallery was very real, a burning feeling in his guts, more acute because he had known they should have killed the guy the moment they found him. He blamed Crane for Jim Gallery's escape. His fool idea about the well had been responsible for that.

Kid Dawson stared into the night, his fist clenched, his fleshy face an ugly mask. He was about to return to the shelter of the cluster of rocks when he thought he saw something move out there in the darkness. He froze. Well, it couldn't be Gallery! The guy wasn't that much of a fool. Maybe this was a trick of the half-light. But there was something! And a moment later he heard the sound of slowly-moving horses, the dull clop-clop of hoofs. Horses! The very thing they needed!

He listened for some moments, disbelieving and then, trailwise, he knew there were two riders. Why were they poking around in this area after sundown? He unfroze – and then hurried back to the others. 'Listen! Horses out there!'

After some moments listening in the silence of the night, there was no doubt, and the hard-cases exchanged glances. The two riders were approaching closer.

'Let's get 'em,' snarled Max Kerle. 'We need mounts.'

'Could be lawmen …'

'The hell it is!'

'Night-riders – now I wonder.' Stephen Crane was being cautious.

Max Kerle was wasting no time. He lay flat behind a convenient boulder, facing the direction of the hoof-falls, his rifle sighted. Taking a tip, the other two adopted the same position. They lay like snakes ready to strike.

The slow clop-clop of shod hoofs came closer, with such caution the waiting men hardly dared breathe. And then the dark outlines of the animals and riders were suddenly visible shapes in the night. Three vicious rifles levelled, sighted and then spoke without mercy, caring nothing about the identity of the victims.

The night was shattered by the sharp crack of the guns. They spat out their deadly, brutal message and the two riders toppled from saddles with almost comical finality. As the reverberations of the guns flashed across the silent land, the horses spooked and raced off. For a moment or two one of the riders had a foot trapped in a stirrup and he was dragged horribly for some distance. This caused the horse to veer and it came right towards the three bushwhackers. That was nice and handy. Kid Dawson made a grab for the trailing leathers. Max Kerle flung his arms around the animal's neck and dragged it to a halt. The crittur jigged in fright but was got under control.

The second animal took some hunting but the three men, determined to succeed, circled the frightened horse. Eventually it was caught, by Kid

Dawson, who figured he was having a triumphant time. The two animals were pacified by horse-wise men and brought back to the cluster of rocks and hobbled, and the saddles and other gear examined. The result was satisfactory; another two rifles in saddle-holsters, with jerky meat and blanket rolls. Then Stephen Crane and Max Kerle went out to look at the two dead men. It was mostly curiosity. It was always possible they might know the rannigans.

They made two big discoveries.

One man was alive. But only just. They didn't care about that.

The second find was more interesting. The almost-dead guy, lean and grim-faced, had two sacks of gold nuggets tied securely around his waist. The sacks of close-woven canvas were fairly heavy and that meant value. Most men would have fixed bags like this to a saddle-horn but it seemed this galoot liked the feel of gold close to him. The find amazed and excited Max Kerle.

'Gold! Heh! Now whadya know!'

As he snatched the sacks from the dying man, the individual moaned and watched them with glittering eyes. Crane and Kerle took a fast look at the other man, now really dead, lying some distance away. And sure enough they found that he, too, was laden with two handy-sized pokes of gold.

The two no-account galoots knew all about gold. Max Kerle had done a spot of panning in his varied career. Crane had gambled for gold.

Stephen Crane turned the dying man over and then propped him up. This was not an act of mercy. He was suddenly blazingly curious.

'Where did you find this gold? Are you prospectors?'

The man stared with pain-wracked eyes. 'No – hell – me and Buddy just picked it up. Get me to a doc.'

'All right,' said Stephen Crane smoothly. 'Tell me more. I'll patch you up. I'm rather good at the medical stuff, you know.'

'Don't let me die ...'

'I won't old man. Now tell me, where did you get the gold if you didn't pan it?'

'Took it – from the old galoot – and his daughter. At the Yellow Stones –'

'Yellow Stones? Where is that?'

'Broken country – just a few miles west o' here. Me an' Buddy was heading back to town.'

'An old man and his daughter? Out here?'

'Yeah, mister – I don't mind tellin' you. Just don't let me die in these badlands. Get me to a doc – I'll tell you anythin'.'

'Keep on talking, fellow,' said Stephen Crane soothingly.

'They've got a mine. Guess there's more gold – you wouldn't believe it – out here – all rock – barren country. We just lit out with four small pokes. Aw, Gawd – don't let me die!'

'You're dead!' snarled Crane in a sudden savage change of tone. He rammed the man back to the ground.

With that, he and Kerle untied the small pokes of gold and carried them away, along with the two from the other man.

Max Kerle was excited. He was thinking: gold – horses! Sheer luck! The kind of luck a range-wanderer dreamed of. Yeah, four small pokes of gold – enough to whet the appetite – two horses – and three men. Did it have to be shared with other bastards no better than himself?

Max Kerle did not realize that Stephen Crane was thinking along the same lines. He was thinking there were one or two men too many in this outfit. But all that would be decided later. Yeah – what was it the dying rider had said about the possibility of more gold?

There was no hiding the finds from Kid Dawson when they got back to the cluster of rocks, the hobbled horses and the other gear that comprised their base. For one thing, Kerle and Crane were so excited they just had to examine the bags of gold again, feel the weight of the nuggets and assess the value.

'More where this came from,' muttered Stephen Crane. 'That dying fool said there was more gold – in some place called Yellow Stones. Do you know about it?'

'Yellow Stones!' Kid Dawson nodded. 'Hell, that ain't far from here – reckon about twenty miles – maybe less. Ain't much now we got hosses.'

'Two horses,' Stephen Crane corrected. 'For three men. Still, no doubt we could reach the place – with you as a guide, amigo!'

Kid Dawson looked at the small pokes of gold. 'Yeah, but what about Gallery?'

'We'll deal with him some day.'

'He could get clear to hell.'

'We'll find him. With gold behind us, we could track down any man.'

'I sure want to kill Gallery – salivate him but good.'

'I like gold as good as revenge.'

'This is sure one lucky night,' leered Max Kerle. 'Four sacks of gold – maybe more to come and –'

The Killer Stamp 43

He very nearly said three men, but that had implications that were better left unsaid.

'We'll set off for this Yellow Stones area at sun-up,' stated Stephen Crane, naturally issuing orders again.

For once the other two men did not make resentful remarks. They began to make camp, hard rannigans but tired with the events of the past hours.

Five

Jim Gallery did not know why he lingered in the place. He had had breakfast, which the girl had cooked for him, a little luxury for a man living on a saddle, and he had shaved, a painful business considering the state of his face. Still, he felt and looked much better, except for the fact that his shirt and pants were a mess. He wet his hair from a jug of cold water Helen brought him from the spring outside and tried to smooth down his thick dark locks. He stared into a mirror; saw the Irish face and grinned at himself. Maybe in a day or two he'd be his old self, ready for some good restaurant food, a drink or two and a hand of cards – but that would be when he was a long way past Delta. There were three hard devils still on his heels.

She came into the living-room and smiled at him. 'My pa seems a lot better already.'

'I guess he's a tough old hombre.'

'He's a hard man,' she admitted. 'He has to be –' She broke off.

Jim Gallery grinned. 'Mining is hard graft, sure thing. Do you like living out here? I mean this barren place is no good for a gal. There's danger –'

'I have to live here with my pa.'

The Killer Stamp

'I didn't know there was gold to be found around here.'

'So you've guessed!' She sighed. 'I might as well tell you – two men rode up and shot my father – not to kill – they wanted to make him talk. To save him further pain, I had to tell them where we had cached some gold – four small pokes – nuggets mostly – dug out of the rock. I don't know how they got to know about us.'

'Stories get around where gold is concerned.'

She regarded him steadily. 'There isn't any more – except in the ground, and the finds are getting scarcer and it's hard work just to win it.'

'You don't have to worry about me. I'm going.'

'I've told you the truth about this place. And you? A man without food or guns or boots? A man with bruises?'

'I've told you. I'm Jim Gallery, just a galoot ridin' by.'

'You're running from other men!'

She had only her intuition. Her comment was so near the truth that Jim grinned ruefully in admission. She saw his expression and turned away, a little disturbed by the presence of this man, so much better looking now that he had cleaned up. She patted her hair; caught sight of her reflection in a mirror and began to think like a woman. Heavens, she needed a new dress! This old gingham thing was so faded! What would he think of her? Did she look plain – or pretty? Perhaps this man had known girls in towns, clever girls and more gracious than she. Heavens, what was stirring in her head? He was just a rough man, riding by!

The next moment there was a growling shout from the bedroom in which her father lay. She hurried to see to him.

Jim Gallery went out to look at the horse. He saddled the animal again after rubbing the crittur down and talking gently to it. He was not in any haste. He stared around the scene. It was in many ways a hideout and right off the beaten track.

It occurred to him that Crane and his sidekicks, if they were pressing on to Delta on foot, would take a trail many miles distant from this place and never give it a thought. They wouldn't be able to track him. In a way, he could lie low here for a few days, taking the girl's hospitality. Maybe it was a good idea.

Looking for Harry Carslake was a long-term job in any case. The robbing, murdering skunk was somewhere in the wild land between the Colorado River and the San Juan River – that he knew from information received – but exactly where he was holed up he wasn't sure about. Certainly not in any town. He had asked a thousand questions of travellers, men he knew, who had taken stage journeys, men who were range-wandering and men dodging the law.

No one had seen Harry Carslake in any town. But he had been seen in the wild sparsely populated land between the rivers, that triangular-shaped chunk of territory where the peaceful Cheyenne and the warlike Apache met. And if he was there, he was hiding, and he would have the twenty thousand dollars which had been formerly part of the big assets of the Drago Cattleman's Bank.

That *dinero* did not belong to Harry Carslake. They had merely lifted it. Al Aston was dead. Harry had killed him. That hadn't been part of the deal. Harry had been told just to get the money and meet Jim Gallery later, but Harry had figured on death and a double-cross.

It was all a set-up that would have to be trimmed with some justice some day. Harry Carslake could not be allowed to get away with it. At the same time, Max Kerle must not be allowed to suspect anything. He didn't even know Harry Carslake.

As Jim rubbed the horse down and tightened the cinch, the girl walked up to him. 'You are leaving?'

'I should move on.'

'You can stay for another meal. I owe you a lot. My father seems a bit improved although his temper is bad. The bleeding has stopped.'

'He'll be all right, Miss Helen.'

'Will you stay?' She seemed eager. Then, realizing she was pressing him, she blushed and lowered her eyes. He knew it was the first time he had seen her lose her composure. He smiled, knowing she was a lovely girl.

'I'll stick around,' he conceded. 'And I'll tell you the story of my life – all the goldarned wicked parts.'

'I don't think you are wicked.'

'Miss, you sure don't know me! I'm the kind who played truant from school – an' it was only open half a day – an' I stole apples. Yeah! And later – well – ah –' He had done too many lawless things which were not a joke. He wouldn't tell her the half of it!

There was the bank robbery, with Max Kerle and Al Aston. She wouldn't like to hear about that! He had killed Kid Dawson's brother – fair and square – but the galoot was dead. Hardly a nice topic of conversation. He had gone for Stephen Crane on account of the bounty. No crime there – but hard stuff. Maybe it had all started way back when his father had been killed during a card game and he had been a youngster. His mother had got in the way of a stagecoach and four horses driven by a drunken ribbon-handler – and he'd taken that hard, unable to understand fate. As a kid he had been kicked around. He had stolen his first gun!

'A penny for them.' She smiled at him.

She was too close, too sweet and clear-skinned for a man who had experienced only Molly Peterson apart from the saloon girls. He impulsively put out a hand and touched the bare skin of her arm. It was like an electric shock just to realize just how lovely and soft she was. His hand stayed on her arm. Looking into her brown eyes, he saw them flicker.

Then he put out his other arm and gathered her into his embrace. In a second she was pressing close to him and his mouth was on her lips, kissing her too savagely.

It was only her struggles some moments later that brought him to his senses. He let her go. Sure, she was beautiful and warm and desirable! Sure, he was a man! He stood, lines biting deeply into his face. 'I'm sorry – I shouldn't have done that.'

'I shouldn't have allowed it –'

'You didn't. I just grabbed. Sorry.'

'I could have slapped your face – but I didn't want to hurt you!'

He laughed. 'After what I've had done to me! I guess I'll have to go now. Just don't think too badly about me.'

'But I don't.'

'I'm not used to girls as pretty and as nice as you.

I'm just a hard-ridin' guy – been hittin' saddle for so long I don't know what decent living is all about. I'll go.'

'Will you come back?' It was an impuslive question which she realized was too daring by far by her western standards. She bit her lip.

'That I might, Helen. I haven't many friends. Maybe I should kinda cultivate some! And you? Don't you ever get into town? They've got two drapery emporiums, I think – kinda interest a gal looking for finery ... And two hotels – with restaurants ...'

'Oh, I've been in a restaurant – with my pa. Yes, it's nice to see people – and other women. We go to church when we're in Delta. We came from Green River country in Wyoming – we did live nicely – we – Oh, I'm talking too much.'

'I've been around Laramie.' He turned to the horse and patted the head. 'You can talk away – I kinda like to hear a gal talkin'. Tell you what – why don't you saddle a nag and ride out with me for some way, huh?'

'You don't want to stay here – for a few days?'

'I'd like to – but –'

He could hardly tell her that he couldn't trust himself when she was close to him – that he might get too fond of her. With three grim men hunting him, he wasn't suitable for a girl like Helen Mackay. He wasn't suitable for any kind of woman. He would have to change a hell of a lot if he wanted roots, a home and a woman.

'Saddle a nag,' he said impulsively.

'I will – right now. I hope Pa will be all right ...'

'He'll be okay.' He bit his lip. 'You won't be away very long. Just ride with me down the trail, huh?'

She nodded again.

He was riding through the rock-filled gullies, away from the half-hidden shack, out towards the open land. Helen Mackay was right behind him. She had taken her horse from their corral and saddled it at the last moment, deciding to see him on his way.

He knew this was the right thing to do. Tempting as it was to stay awhile, he also realized the dangers. He might want to grab the girl again! And somewhere there were three hard cases who wanted his blood.

She wasn't riding side-saddle this time but astride, which was more suited to the life she was leading out here in the badlands, away from civilization. She wore blue jeans and a checked shirt and seemed more feminine as a result. They rode behind the last of the giant rock sentinels, with the thorny cactus at the base, and paused for a moment.

He let the girl continue talking. He was watching the dark speck of a lone rider on a distant slope of the land.

He reined in and Helen followed suit, silent now. They waited. The man and horse were making directly for the thrust of rocks. As the horse plodded on, the rider seemingly patient, he could see the blotch of white on the nag's head bobbing regularly. There was also something familiar about the man's shape. And then he knew.

This man now approaching them was the sheriff of Delta, one Mack Slater, a tubby galoot with an honest way of dealing with his problems.

What the devil brought him out here? What was behind his direct approach to the broken rocky

The Killer Stamp

land? Who was he looking for? A lawman wouldn't ride all this way just for fun, not in this heat and over this hard terrain. He wasn't passing the time of day. Mack Slater had something on his mind. One thing was for sure; the man did not have anything on one Jim Gallery, no knowledge of his lawless past because there was nothing on record. And he had been a good boy when in Delta.

'See him?' said Jim softly. 'The sheriff ...'

Six

The three hard guys were for the time being in a good humour as they rode slowly over the undulating arid lands. They even bandied jokes, each in their own manner, with coarseness from Max Kerle and some subtle comments from Stephen Crane – which were lost on the others. Kid Dawson rode up behind the Englishman on one horse and Max Kerle enjoyed the comfort of a saddle to himself. The dozen or so miles to the Yellow Stones district was going to be pleasant. There was, it seemed, some tonic effect in the very feel of a poke of gold. Two were slung from Stephen Crane's saddle pommel and two with Max Kerle. The men were trusting each other – temporarily!

The sun climbed steadily, causing heat shimmers to dance on the horizon. The ride was a slow one, stopping repeatedly so that the horses could be given a drink from canteens. At this moment in time, to the three rannies, the cayuses were mighty important. All the same, they regaled themselves with water. They still had plenty of hard ground to traverse and memory of the footsore trek from the Indian well was still with them.

'Gold, huh!' Max Kerle bawled. 'Ain't that

somethin', Kid?'

'Seems good.'

'Possibly more at this Yellow Stones place,' remarked Stephen Crane. 'It's worth looking into, I'd say.'

'Howsabout the old galoot and his daughter? Like that dying feller said – there's an old man and his gal.'

'If they give any trouble,' said Stephen Crane coldly, 'we shall have to eliminate them. What else?'

'I don't get it why them two rannigans didn't take all the gold while they was at it,' pursued Max Kerle. 'I mean, Crane, how do we know there's more?'

'That man said there was more. He was dying.'

'Sure – an' maybe he was just talking wild. I just don't figure why they didn't take all the gold – that's all.'

'He said more where it came from,' ruminated Stephen Crane. 'I suppose that could mean anything.'

'Yeah – maybe he was crazy with pain …'

'Well, do we look at this Yellow Stones place – or press on to Delta and what passes for civilization in this confounded country?'

'You puttin' this to the vote an' not issuing orders as usual?' asked Max Kerle sarcastically.

'I'd like to plug Jim Gallery,' hissed Kid Dawson. A mask-like twist settled on his fleshy face. He was working up to his hate again. 'He'll be ahead of us all the way if we stop off at this Yellow Stones place. Maybe we got enough gold?'

'A man can never accumulate enough gold,' sneered the ex-army man. 'Damn, if I really struck it rich – I mean real wealth – I'd sail for England

and buy myself a proper estate befitting my previous position in life. Do you know what it is like to have servants only too glad to obey one's slightest whim? Could you appreciate the theatre in London or the exclusiveness of a good gentlemen's club? I doubt it.'

'We ain't got your education – Colonel – sir –'

'My ma was educated. She could read,' said Kid Dawson.

'But you never knew who your pa was!' Max Kerle threw back and roared with laughter.

The two horses were moving steadily, climbing a long gradual rise of the land, going in the direction indicated by Kid Dawson, who insisted he knew where to find the Yellow Stones location. As they breasted the long incline, the horses were halted while Max Kerle pointed a long dirty-sleeved arm to the bed of the valley below.

'Hell and tarnation – look at that!'

The sandy bed, with its generous tufts of bunch grass, indicating water somewhere, bore a dark patch right in the centre. About fifty horses were placidly grouped together in a large circle and cropping at the scarce bunch grass. There were solids, big blacks and brown, and there were some multi-coloured mustangs. The solids were big horses, about fifteen hands high, and the others were smaller, wiry critturs. A man on a saddle horse sat hunched, apparently watching the *remuda*, content to sit out there in the sun. To one side, in the shade of a large boulder, a smaller figure sat. After a second glance by the three men on the rise, they came to the conclusion that the smaller figure was a boy. He was wearing a floppy Stetson, miles too big for him, and dusty range gear. The man on the saddle horse wore a buckskin jacket – which must have been warm for him – and black pants tucked into scuffed boots.

No more details were apparent to the three hard cases on the rise. Distance blurred the view. But probably the man on the saddled horse, watching the herd, wore a gunbelt and hardware to suit. He didn't turn his mount or even move, so they could not be sure.

'Now don't that take some beatin'!' exclaimed Max Kerle. 'What the devil are they doin' out there with a pack of horseflesh like that?'

'That's a neat question,' said Stephen Crane. 'Seeing that this is the fringe of the badlands! Who would want to drive a *remuda* in this direction? He's off the proper trail.'

'Maybe he's lost ...' This contribution from Kid Dawson. 'Looks like a mustanger with his son. Say, I hear there's plenty of hosses in the San Juan Mountains.'

'There's plenty right here,' said Max Kerle wickedly. 'Can you figure what they're worth, partner? I can see two that look real beauts! Worth a hundred dollars each in the right market. You know that, Kid?'

'I know hosses,' said the other defensively.

'Fifty prime mounts –, an' only a man an' his son,' murmured Max Kerle. 'Say, this badland country is mighty interesting! First it's gold – and now a collection of prime horseflesh!'

'Have we got time?' Stephen Crane twisted in his saddle. 'Hell, we want to look at this gold worked by some old man and his girl – and then we want to obliterate Gallery.'

'We can do the lot.'

Kid Dawson protested. 'What the hell are you gettin' at, Kerle? You figure to steal that damned *remuda*?'

'We could do with another mount,' argued the lanky ruffian. 'And a few spare hosses is always a good idea – so why not take the lot?'

'What the hell!'

'I tell you that pack of critturs is worth *dinero*. All we have to do is drive them to Delta – an' we don't want the mustanger and his kid around to argue otherwise when we hit town.'

Stephen Crane nodded. 'All is grist that comes to the mill.'

'What the hell does that mean?'

'We could drive them to Yellow Stones and take a day off to look into this gold prospect. Then it's an easy trail to Delta, huh?'

'Oh, goddamit – what about Gallery?' yelled the Kid. 'Ain't we after that bastard or not? I want to string him up an' use him as target practice! If we fool around, he'll get plumb away to hell and gone!'

'We've got time,' said the army man. 'You have no patience, my man. Have you forgotten the weeks it has taken us to track Gallery in any case? Another week won't matter. We'll get him, rest assured. You'll have your revenge.'

'Yeah – well don't talk to me like I was some fool woman!'

Max Kerle patted his horse. Not that he had any sympathy with the animal. It was simply a crittur that obeyed commands – or else. 'Let's ride down nice an' easy like. We don't want to scare 'em. We're just three honest Joes that's lost a horse – an' maybe we'd like to buy one – and we're heading for Delta and our humble families. That sound good, Crane?'

'Slightly nauseating – but I know you, Kerle. Yes, let's ride down, slowly, easily, and we'll get the man's story – before we deal with the fool and the boy.'

'Dead folks don't tell no tales,' muttered the hawklike man.

With Kid Dawson grumbling incoherently about the wasted time, the two animals plodded down into the valley. Max Kerle waved in friendly salute to the mustanger. When they were closer, Stephen Crane shouted a greeting. 'Hello, my friend! You seem to be off-trail with your herd. Are you bound for Delta? We're three wanderers and we've lost a horse. How about selling us a mount?'

The man in the buckskin jacket stared with a long look; then he nudged his horse forward and nodded. At the same time the slight figure rose from the shade of the boulder. The floppy old Stetson was pushed back to reveal fair curly hair. Max Kerle was the first to make comment. 'By heck, it's a gal!'

'I'm Delia Breen – and this is my father – known to most as Walt.' The girl regarded them with a steady expression.

The mustanger was a man of about forty-five, it seemed to the three hard-cases. He was dark-bearded and broad-shouldered, a solid man. He said: 'We ain't off-trail, mister. I ain't that stupid. Truth is we've driven these cayuses in a wide loop. I've been hunting mustangs in the San Juan hills and buying some other stock here and there. We had a deal to sell 'em in Silverton but that fell through, so I figured to skirt these badlands and get to Delta. The cavalry agent is in Delta an' looking for good mounts.'

'Yeah — fifteen hands for a cavalry mount,' said Max Kerle knowingly.

'Sure — wal, I got some good ones right here. Them solids should sell. The mustangs are good, too — make good cowponies for the ranchers west of Delta ...'

'You and your daughter have driven these animals all this way?' This question, spoken pleasantly, from Stephen Crane.

'Sure. Delia's as good as any man with these critturs.'

Stephen Crane almost bowed. His eyes swept appreciatively over the girl's figure. No one noticed the cold look deep in those eyes. 'I'm sure she is very capable, Mr Breen. And very pretty, I'm sure — if she was dressed in womanly clothes.'

'Delia don't worry none about her gear,' said the mustanger. 'She's a good girl ...'

'I'm sure she is,' Crane was very polite. No one could read the sudden unspeakable desires in his ugly mind as he looked at this girl in the absurd clothes. The youthful quality, hidden in dusty jeans, shirt and ragged buckskin vest, was something he felt he should possess by fair means or foul. She was suddenly a prize for the taking.

'Howsabout selling us a hoss, mister?' Max Kerle jerked. It was merely a play. He was waiting for some sign from Crane.

'Sure, why not, if we can agree on price,' said Walt Breen. 'Why don't we sit down, light a fire and have a bite to eat an' some coffee? I was just thinking on this — seeing the animals are nicely settled.'

As if he was agreeable to the prospect of company, the man got down from his saddle. He

The Killer Stamp

walked about three yards, intending to go to the stack of provisions which had been dumped near the boulder.

Stephen Crane whipped out his Colt .45 and pointed it at the mustanger. 'You are, my man, unfortunately in our way. I regret this action but some people are expendable.'

For a few seconds the other man froze, his hand a long way from his gun. 'Now see here, mister – you ain't got no right ...'

With cold-blooded deliberation Crane fired his gun at point-blank range, the killer stamp suddenly on his face. The Colt roared death.

Walt Breen toppled slowly forward, trying to stand upright. Hellish pain tore through him and whipped away in seconds his very life force. He fell face down, dying, sliding so slowly to the earth, and at the same time Delia's scream of shock and fear tore through the air. The mustanger's horse jibbed in fright. The pack of horses wheeled a bit and Max Kerle, along with the Kid went to pacify the animals, Kid Dawson now off Crane's mount and moving swiftly on foot.

Delia crouched over her father's body. That he was dead there could be no doubt. Crane's gun had sent a slug into the heart. She leaned over the man who had been protector all her young life. Cries of horror at the sight of blood screamed from her throat.

Grinning evilly, the killer stamp now so apparent, Crane slid from his horse and walked closer to the girl. She rose like a fury and went for him with eye-gouging fingers. He had to use all his strength to beat her off. Then with a quick new thought she dived to the boulder where lay the provisions.

Stephen Crane was no slouch where threats to his skin were concerned. He saw the danger. He saw the leather belt and the gun which was lying near the grubstake. So the girl wore a gun most of the time! It was a good bet she was adept at using it! A spirited filly, no less. But he would tame her!

His big strides took him to the boulder at the same time that the girl got there. He grabbed roughly at the gunbelt and pushed the girl to one side. She hit her head on the side of the boulder and lay dazed for a few seconds. The time element was enough for Crane to throw the gunbelt safely to one side.

When the girl recovered her wits, she saw this man crouching over her, his face a mask of lust and cunning. Gone was the façade of the gentleman. In that moment Stephen Crane was revealed for what he was; an inhuman beast!

'Don't worry, my dear,' he sneered. 'You will be taken care of. I am a fine man, a person of some distinction. Stephen Crane is the name, an officer and a gentleman. You know, you are a very lovely girl – even in grief – although why you are crying I do not know. He is simply a dead man now. God, there is something of the gamine in you! How interesting!'

She clawed at him again, screaming abuse. 'You murderer! You dirty killer! Oh, my poor pa! You have killed him!'

He was holding her, enjoying in some cruel manner the way she fought him, when Max Kerle and the Kid returned from calming the horses. They stood near to Stephen Crane and the girl and laughed.

'Say, what do you figure to do with her?' Kid

The Killer Stamp

Dawson guffawed. 'Looks like we'll have to shoot her, too, Steve.'

The army man slapped the girl's face harshly with some idea of calming her and then he rose to his feet. His boots firmly planted among the sand and rock chips, he said: 'You are a fool, Dawson. And do not address me as "Steve" – unless you want me to break your neck. The girl will be protected by me – for the time being, anyway.'

'Protected, hell! We got plenty on our hands. We don't want a damned girl!'

'Look, my man – it's a long time since I had a girl. Those whores in town are not quite the same.'

'Yeah, she sure looks purty,' mocked Max Kerle.

Her old Stetson had fallen off to reveal a mass of corn-coloured curls, lovely enough to turn any man's head. Her womanly shape showed through the dusty check shirt.

'Seems our colonel is mighty attracted to this bit of female,' went on Max Kerle. 'And I can't say I rightly blame him – except our colonel, sir, is just a bit too long in the tooth for this filly. But there's fun in taming, I guess.'

He got a hard stare from Crane for his taunts but that did not disconcert Max Kerle. He had his secret thoughts, too. He did not bawl out the first thing that entered his head, unlike Kid Dawson.

There was the gold – so went his secret thoughts – and a two-way share was better than three. But better still if it went the way of only one man! Then there was the pack of horseflesh. Sure, it was worth *dinero* in the right place but fifty animals needed some handling all the way to Delta. Too many for one man.

And now a girl! She wasn't worth money but

pleasures always cost a price. It had been a long time since he had last had a woman. This young girl looked a real peach. Trouble was, Crane had the same thoughts.

'We don't need the girl,' yelled Kid Dawson.

'Should ha' figured you'd be keen to get a hold on her,' sneered Kerle. 'What's the matter, Kid? Lost the zest?'

'We gotta look in at the mine at Yellow Stones.'

'Yeah – we can do all that.'

'And how about pushin' on for Gallery? Hell, we started out with the intention of killing that skunk.'

'He'll keep, you dumb fool.' Max Kerle showed all his contempt for the younger man.

'How are we goin' to explain this gal when we hit Delta?'

'Let me take care of those details,' said Crane coldly. 'This girl will go along with us – for the time being.'

'Aw, I get you. Just for the time being ... then we shoot her, huh?'

'Maybe.' Stephen Crane assumed his old voice of authority. 'How far are we from this Yellow Stones area, Dawson?'

'Sure ain't far. Just a few miles. I'll recognize the place when we get near it.'

'We'll drive the horses over there. We might be able to find a rough corral among the rocks – if the terrain is as broken as you say, Dawson.'

'It's sure rough. Big rocks standing like barns – an' there's gullies – all in this yellow stone – it's sandstone, I guess.'

'Then we corral the *remuda* and look into this question of further gold. That won't take long.'

'You figure to plug the old galoot and his

daughter when we get there?' sneered Max Kerle. 'Not that a bit of shootin' throws me, pard.'

Stephen Crane glared. 'Pard, indeed! So damned uncouth! Never mind – yes, we'll kill them if we have to.'

'And you'll corral that gal, too – the one at the gold mine, huh?'

'If she is worth any attention.'

'By God, Crane – you gotta appetite!'

'For the good things in life, you mean?' Crane ran his eyes over the crying girl again. 'Yes, there are certain lusts in a man – the need for money, women, drink, a good hand of cards. I admit to liking all these carnal pleasures.'

'And, hell, how you talk!' sneered the other man. 'Just like as we was some dirt under them boots o' yourn, huh, Crane?'

'Don't attempt to be clever, Kerle.'

The other man turned away. 'Wal, we've got a pack of work to do. Hope you aim to do your share of it, Crane.'

Kid Dawson blustered up. 'Look, Mister Crane – leave that gal – or salivate her. Sure as hell she'll be trouble.'

'You will obey orders, Dawson.'

The command had all the air of authority and left Kid Dawson staring and ill-tempered. But the time for word-play was over because there was work to do.

Delia Breen backed to the shelter of the boulder, wishing she could kill this tall hateful man with the greying hair and moustache, while the other two men saw to their mounts. Kid Dawson took the mustanger's saddled animal, jerking at the leathers to assure himself that everything was OK and holding the head harness.

Max Kerle circled the group of horses, noting appreciatively their good qualities. This string of broomtails was worth money, especially in Delta, where the army agent was buying, if the rumours were correct. He came right back to where Crane was standing, watching the girl, a nasty twist to his lips.

'We're ready to go,' said Max Kerle.

'She's got a mount hidden in the shade of that big rock,' said the other man. 'Watch her while I secure the animal.'

Crane strode off. The girl eyed Kerle as if she wished him dead. Then she began to move slowly.

'You ain't goin' anywhere,' Kerle issued the warning.

'Am I not allowed to move – to walk?'

'All right.' He grinned, eyes watching her nastily. 'Walk. You look good walkin'.'

She moved slowly, uncertainly, around him and he watched with unpleasant amusement. His eyes were practically unclothing her. He saw wild grace in her limbs and knew Crane was right. She had some youthful style in that slender body.

And then she dived like a wild creature for her father's body – and the gun still stuck in his holster.

Max Kerle was really late in starting his reaction, and as he dived at her, she whipped the gun out of leather, really fast. She was slick with a Colt, he discovered, even though the weapon looked like a small cannon in her hand. The gun barked ferociously and the flame flashed almost in Max Kerle's face. He felt the hiss of the slug as it cut air only inches from his head.

Then he was struggling with the lithe girl,

grabbing at the Colt and wrenching it from her grasp before she could fire again. He flung the gun away, yelling his anger. She made an instinctive attempt to dive after it but he grabbed her, held her in a vicious hug that nearly cracked her ribs. For some seconds she stared into his furious, dirty, bewhiskered visage, glaring back defiantly at him. Then when he knew he had bested the girl, he kept her in the tight embrace and chuckled triumphantly as she regarded him with loathing.

'Let me go – you killer – you dirt!'

'Wal, now, I'm right happy just holdin' you like a frisky filly, Miss Delia Breen ...'

'You awful brute!' She screamed, the feminine cry cutting the air.

'Get your stinking hands off her!'

The grating command right behind him was rough with animosity. Max Kerle looked up to see the angry expression on Stephen Crane's face. Eyes bored into each other. Kerle gave way.

'Why, this gal tried to kill me! Just went for her old pa's gun! I was mighty lucky to dodge that slug. Yessir!'

A hand like a vice descended on Kerle's shoulder and rammed him back. The girl pushed away from them. She watched in some fear as Max Kerle faced the man who considered himself superior.

'You sore about somethin'?' Max Kerle's sneer was an insult in itself. 'You figure to take all the cake – Colonel – Sir?'

'Leave – her – alone!' The hissed command was full of real menace. 'That's an order. I mean it, Kerle.'

Kid Dawson watched the other two men with a kind of irritation. He had a one-track mind. The chores that lay ahead nagged at him. And the girl was a nuisance. He felt if a man wanted a woman, there were the brothel girls in any town.

'Are you two out of your minds?' His full face was creased in anger. 'I've a doggone mind to take my share of the gold and light out for Gallery on my own.'

'You do that, Kid. You go right ahead. Ask the General for your share. You can't do anything without the Colonel's permission.'

There were angry muttered comments from all the men and then they turned to the horses. Crane brought the girl's small mare from the nook where it had been tethered. He then told Kerle – giving orders again – to tie the girl's hands together in front of her while he held her shoulders. She struggled; certainly not the kind of girl to submit meekly. But with two rough men there was no chance. She was then helped to vault to her saddle. Crane made a lead rope from the coil which was looped on his mount and tied one end to the leathers of the small mare. Then he got to his saddle and watched her with a cold smile as if she was his personal captive.

Kid Dawson, under instruction, took as much of the grubstake which had belonged to the mustanger as he could tie around his newly acquired mount. Then he and Max Kerle rode out wide to circle the pack of horses while Stephen Crane, with the girl's mount on a lead rope, rode drag. In this manner, they got the pack moving, slowly because they did not wish to spook them.

After some miles, when they were used to the pack and the vagaries of two horses in particular, they were moving nicely. Walking horses moved faster than a cattle herd. They made good progress, and then Kid Dawson gave a shout and pointed to the horizon.

'That's the Yellow Stones! Always figured they was just rock and cactus. Just a hideout for sidewinders. Not many men went near the Yellow Stones – so I heard.'

'Wal, we aim to,' said Max Kerle. 'If there's more gold, we sure want it.'

'Greedy, ain't we? Wal, I'll take gold – but this gal – and maybe this pack of horseflesh – is too much –'

The pile-up of rock lay like a yellowish tinge on the sky line, becoming larger and more definite as they drove the horses over the undulating, chaparral-studded land. The lack of water in this area was so obvious.

When they got real close to the weathered stands of rock, they looked like a natural corral. In a place like this there was nearly always a blind canyon or basin where animals could be herded. They found a large recess which took the pack. They rolled some boulders closer, not without some grumbles about the work. Kid Dawson elected to stand guard while the other two rode real deep into the Yellow Stones.

They had been gone about half an hour, and he was cursing the heat and brooding about Jim Gallery, when he was startled by a flurry of gunshots. They cracked the silent air unexpectedly, like some warning – was it of disaster? The gunshots came from inside the rocky maze. Had Crane and Kerle come across the prospector and the girl and killed them?

If so, that was fast work, but knowing Stephen

Crane anything could have happened. But what about the gold? Why start shooting before information about the gold was forthcoming?

Kid Dawson rolled a cigarette, smoked grimly and waited.

Seven

Jim Gallery watched the figure of Mack Slater ride up and halt his elderly horse. The man pushed back his hat and used his red bandanna to mop his brow.

'Sure is plenty hot among these rocks,' he said cheerfully.

Jim Gallery waited. He noted the careful appraisal which the sheriff gave him. Then it came: 'I've seen you in Delta, mister.'

'I've been there …'

'What brings you out here, Sheriff?' Helen Mackay asked.

'Two wandering hellions, Miss. You know a lawman hears more in the saloons than he'll ever get handed to him if he tramped the town asking questions day and night. Now I heard some darned disturbing news last night. Seems two hard cases came out this way to look for gold – your gold, Miss. Oh, sure, folks in Delta know your pa struck a nice little find out here – not that anyone expected gold among these darned rocks.'

'You are too late,' said Helen bitterly. 'Two men did ride in here last night. They stole all the loose gold and dust my pa has worked for over the months – and even shot him.'

'Shot him? Is he bad?'

'Not too ill, thankfully. This man – Jim Gallery – was camped on the trail and he helped me. My pa was bleeding badly from the wound.'

'You were near here last night?' Mack Slater turned shrewd eyes on Jim. He sat hunched, easy in his saddle, his thumbs hooked into his belt, his clean tan shirt bulging a little across a generous stomach. 'You like spendin' the nights in these wild parts, friend?'

'Nope. I like towns.' Jim Gallery grinned. 'I like food that some other galoot has cooked and I like a nice clean chintz tablecloth.'

'Some feller hit you lately?'

'A man in Delta.'

'Fightin' don't do a man much good,' observed the sheriff and he shook his head sadly. 'In Delta you say?'

'Yep ...'

'Funny. When I saw you ride out you sure looked mighty handsome – not a bruise in sight and not a trace of a black eye. And you were sitting a different hoss. I was watching you. I watch all kinds of gents – an' some of the ladies. You weren't in Delta for any kind of work or business ...'

'Just a drifter. You must get plenty,' drawled Jim, smiling at the man's probing.

Mack Slater nodded. 'Wal, it don't signify none. You want me to take a look at your pa, Miss Helen? I know plenty about wounds.'

'Well, a second opinion might be a good idea – and my pa likes you. He'd love to talk.'

'I'll ride back with you, Helen,' said Jim Gallery. 'Then maybe when the sheriff is set to return to Delta, I'll go with him. Mighty good thing to have

The Killer Stamp

the law riding alongside.'

In actual fact, Helen prepared a meal for the sheriff and he helped himself to generous lashings of coffee. Bert Mackay walked stiffly into the room and seemed eager to talk with the sheriff. Jim Gallery settled back, watching Helen, thinking that this young woman was a real beauty. Was he being too impressed? If she knew the truth about him, the hard trails he had traversed, the truth about the Drago Cattleman's Bank robbery – well, a man should not dwell on the grim facts of life out here in the west.

'They was two damned town scum!' snapped Bert Mackay. 'They came bustin' in and demanded gold. The skunks shot me just to prove they weren't fooling!'

'Not those two,' remarked the sheriff. 'You were dealing with hell-bent cusses. They're not really Delta men – just scum that drifted in, as you say.'

'I hope that gold is a curse to 'em!' roared Bert. 'Damn their hides! If I was fit, I'd ride after them.'

'I'll look around – but they'll be heading for freedom in any direction now. Wal, this is mighty nice apple pie, Miss Helen.' Mack Slater licked his lips. 'I'll put out wanted posters for them two gents that robbed you, Bert, not that there's much chance of finding them – and it ain't much of a description – an' I reckon they'll hightail it for some outlandish place where they can sell the gold. Maybe they'll drink themselves to death, huh? Gold always brings grief, anyway.'

'Damn them! I've a good mind to ride out.'

'You're not fit, Mr Mackay,' said Jim Gallery quietly. 'That wound wouldn't allow you to get far.'

'Pa – you can't ride out!'

'I'll mosey around,' announced Mack Slater, 'but I can't travel far. There's things to take care of in town. Judge Petter is holding a court tomorrow and I got to be there – an' I got some drunks in the cells.'

'Thanks for riding out to warn us,' said the girl, 'but it's too late, of course.'

The sheriff rose to go, refreshed after the coffee and the liberal food. Jim Gallery went with him to the tie-rail outside. They got to saddle leather; spent a few more minutes talking to Helen and Bert Mackay and then left, moving along the rocky defile that led out of the Yellow Stones. The last Jim Gallery saw of the girl, she was waving goodbye to him. He twisted back in his saddle, a twinge of regret in his mind. Well, maybe he would return. Damnit, he would return!

He had Harry Carslake on his mind and the three hellions he had left way back in the area near the old Indian well. That they would trail him – or at least reach Delta – he had no doubt. They had guns, food and water and maybe only legs, but they were experienced trail-hands. Horses were very often there for the taking to toughs who did not mind being branded horse-thieves. Sure, they'd hit Delta.

Mack Slater suddenly asked in his sly old way: 'You just rode out here, young feller, and camped somewheres out in the open, and then Miss Helen found you?'

'That's the way of it.'

'Ain't much reason,' said the sheriff shrewdly.

'Wal, maybe –'

'And you ain't toting a gun. Now when you left Delta you was all fixed up with Colt an' rifle.'

'I know. You saw me ...'

'Sure thing. That's the way I do things. I just mosey around and keep an eye open.'

Jim Gallery smiled thinly. He would put up with the middle-aged sheriff's rumbling comments, his attempts to pump him, until they reached town and then, after trading the horse for another animal and buying some new gear, he'd ride out on the long search for Harry Carslake and the missing money. For that little investigation he'd need guns.

They rode through twisting gullies, where tall rocks stood up on all sides like jagged teeth and the green cholla cactus filled many a hole and crevice. They had nearly reached the open land when they suddenly spotted the approaching two horses and riders.

The recognition was swift. Stephen Crane and Max Kerle, mounted! How the hell had they managed that? Who had they killed for the beasts?

A big hunk of rock, standing like a crazy monument that had been fashioned by wind and rain, was nearby. Jim Gallery jigged his horse immediately into the cover. 'In here, Sheriff! Them hombres ...'

He was too late. A hail of fire spurted from the guns of the two oncoming riders and Mack Slater was caught in it. A slug tore into his chest, jerking him back on the saddle with a harsh cry of pain and fear. Another bullet made a bloody hole in his forehead, and the swift onslaught tore the life out of him and he began to topple as his horse jigged and pranced in fright.

Jim Gallery was in the cover of the fantastically-shaped spire of rock. As Mack Slater hit the ground, he dashed out, grabbed the dying man and dragged him to the rock. The sheriff was a dead man with those wounds; a flashing glance was all that was needed to check that. Jim took the man's Colt, held it angrily, crouched. He whipped a glance at the horse as it slewed in a futile prancing circle. The animal came closer to where Jim Gallery crouched, gun in hand, his other hand holding his own animal's leathers. The sheriff's animal was fairly near and he thought the rifle in the saddle holster would be a great asset – if he could get it!

He darted for the cayuse, thinking to get the animal before the crittur veered away again in a fresh burst of fight. He wanted that rifle. As he came out in the open, more slugs from hand guns spat furiously at him and kicked up dust and rock chips – but not one killer slug hit him!

Jim tugged hastily at the rifle, grabbed at the horse's trailing reins and then dived back for cover. The animal came willingly with him. He looped the leathers around a jagged outcrop of rock; then attended to his own horse in the same fashion and took a swift stock of his surroundings.

He was all right as long as Crane and Kerle stayed where they were in the defile. But if they figured to climb the nearby tall rocks they could get above him. And, indeed, circle him. Two galoots with death to hand out could always cook up an advantage over one.

He did not spend much time wondering how they had got mounts. He had seen instantly they were not the horses he had driven off miles from the Indian well.

Jim Gallery edged to the corner of the huge rock; tried a couple of random shots in the general

The Killer Stamp 75

direction of the two men and then desisted. He would have to save his ammunition. He couldn't reload. He had no spare slugs. Judging by the feel of the rifle, it was fully loaded.

If he could kill Stephen Crane and Max Kerle in this little ruckus, that would not cause him the slightest regret. In fact, it was a matter of the survival of the fittest.

It wasn't entirely unexpected when he heard raging shouts from the two men. 'You – Gallery – so this is where you got to!' That was Max Kerle, full of fury. 'You're one tricky hombre – but we'll leave you for buzzard bait this time!'

Jim Gallery decided to benefit from an exchange of verbal shots. 'How did you know I was here?'

'We didn't!' came Stephen Crane's cool retort. 'We rode in here for other reasons – but we're certainly glad to catch up with you. It couldn't be better. We have the advantage, Gallery. Two to one! We'll leave you for dead this time.'

'You know what you've done?' yelled Jim. 'You've shot the sheriff from Delta – one Mack Slater. He's dead.'

'Now ain't that too bad,' came Max Kerle's sneering remark.

'He was respected in town. The folks back there don't like killers – not your stamp.'

'Gallery, you know we don't give a damn! Kerle and I are going to kill you, too. I dislike you more than ever. You have repeatedly tried to best me. First by handing me over for bounty money – damn your nerve – and then tricking us at the Indian well. Kerle has his reasons for hating your guts – mainly money.'

'Aw, the hell with this yap!' The hoarse yell came

from Max Kerle. 'Let's salivate this gink! That's what we want — him dead as a corpse for the buzzards. We got other things to do.'

Jim Gallery wondered where Kid Dawson was placed. Was he with them? Strange that he should be silent. No — the Kid must be elsewhere. As Crane had yelled, they were two to one. Probably at the mouth of the Yellow Stones. Maybe he was on the lookout.

He realized he had to get above the other two men before they did the same to him. With a quick look around, he leaped for a rising hillock of sand, shale and cactus that rose just to his left. At the top of the hillock a pinnacle of rock stood like a giant's tooth. This would be a good vantage-point.

As he moved shots barked at him and came unpleasantly near, a grim feeling. The slugs dug into the earth all around him but he was leaping, moving like a frantic animal and he was a difficult target. He jumped to a boulder, rested for a moment or two and then darted lithely to another rock. The last part was the most difficult. He had to race up a shale slope where there was no cover. He attracted a hail of slugs. Seemed the others had plenty of ammunition! Some guy was using a rifle, too, and that he did not like. He dug his heels into the soft slope, sending shale slithering down, and he dived like a madman for the pinnacle.

He reached cover, hugged the rock for some time and then sighted his rifle. It was good to have the feel of a big gun again. He saw the black shape of Max Kerle down below, just to one side of the big outcrop of rock. He fired, two quick shots. He missed the man and swore because this was not some fool game he was in. He wanted to kill. He had to kill. Max Kerle dived for new cover, yelling furiously, his cursing cries echoing in the defile.

Jim Gallery bit his lip. He was short of ammunition. Sure, he had the guns – but no spare slugs for them. He'd have to watch it. If the other two realized his shortage, they would play with him, make him waste shots. Well, there was only one answer; he'd have to get in a killer shot. Or at least wound a man. But they would not scare easily.

Down in the defile, Max Kerle rapped across to Stephen Crane: 'He's above us, the tricky swine! Moved fast! Now why'n hell did he stop by in this place, huh?

'Perhaps he intended it for a hideout instead of Delta.'

'We'll have to move out – get around him,' muttered Max Kerle. 'Heck, seems we killed a lawman.'

'Does that matter?' Crane dismissed the fact.

But Max Kerle was using his cunning brain, thinking somebody might get shot to bits here. Just when there's gold a-plenty. Hell, that made a man think. Sure, he hated Jim Gallery but, as Crane had said, it was all *dinero*. There had been the suspicion that Gallery had done him out of the Drago loot by some means, but proof had been lacking, leaving only lousy suspicions.

A man didn't want to die when he had his hands on gold. A man didn't want to die at any time, except that there were things he had to face up to, insults and grievances he wouldn't swallow.

Now if Crane got himself killed trying to buzzard-bait Gallery, no one would lose much sleep. With Crane out of the way, the gold would go much further. Even the pack of horses could be handled by the Kid and himself.

'Are we going to move out and get that jigger?' Max Kerle asked. He eyed the other man furtively. Would Crane take chances and thereby stop a slug? Or was it best to successfully polish off Gallery and stick with his partner – until the gold was ready to be shared?

'Move around him,' muttered Stephen Crane. 'Use the rifles. All we need is one good shot and that saddletramp will be out of our hair.'

Leaving the horses tied in a rocky nook, the two men separated and began climbing carefully among the debris of rocks that littered this broken land. They hoped to get the edge on Gallery; get around him and get a glimpse of him for just long enough to snap off a fast accurate shot.

Max Kerle looked backwards, sombrely, at the horses and the significant little pokes of gold tied around the saddles. There was real spending money there, readily exchangeable in any frontier town for the good things of life – drink, gambling and a woman or two!

He looked carefully ahead, at the slope of shale and the pinnacle of rock which sheltered that hardcase, Gallery. The tricky rannigan was lying low, pretty silent.

'Waitin', huh!' muttered Max Kerle. 'Or maybe he ain't got too much lead for them smoke poles ...'

He crawled around a boulder and then decided to dart to another. As he rushed forward, hunched, his dirty boots scuffing into loose soil and shale, Jim Gallery spotted him and chanced two shots. Max Kerle swore viciously as the bullets stung the ground close to him, and his final movement was a desperate dive to the boulder, where he lay dragging in breath, his face close to the warm rock. The gritty dust stuck to the saliva on his lips. His fingers gripped his rifle tightly with rage.

'Damn you, Gallery! By hell, I'll get you in the end!'

Stephen Crane was taking a wide loop that would bring him up behind Jim Gallery, so that the lean man would have to contend with fire from two directions. Crane's movements took time to accomplish, but that was an essential of good tactics. He made a difficult climb up some ledges of rock, which made him pant a bit, but then he was ready. Gallery was below him, a prize target, hugging the tooth-like pinnacle, watching Max Kerle. Crane sighted his rifle. He was an excellent shot, army-trained in the use of firearms and accurate when given time to aim.

He sighted deliberately, sure that he would now kill Jim Gallery. He wasn't going to miss this easy target. This was the end of the trail for the annoying swine, a man who had bested him in the past.

Crack! Crack!

The second shot was delayed and almost unnecessary. Jim Gallery jerked like some animal impaled by an agonizing knife. He then fell face forward and lay still.

Stephen Crane could not resist an exultant shout. 'Got him!' And then he stood up and waved his gun.

Max Kerle rose from the boulder which was sheltering him as if he was some kind of ground rat. He stood up and yelled at his partner. 'You sure? You gutted the swine?'

'I got him.'

'Yippee! Ain't that the good news! Say, let's take a look.'

'If you feel that's necessary.'

Both men began to converge on the tall pinnacle of rock at the base of which lay Jim's body.

They were out in the open, boots digging roughly into the loose earth as they climbed the slope, when the deep bark of rifles sounded behind them and bullets hissed angrily around them. The two startled men leaped for cover. More shots spat into the ground close to them.

Away down the defile, on a flat shelf of rock, Helen Mackay and her father stood openly and pumped shell after shell at the two scoundrels.

'The hell!' Max Kerle. 'What now? Aw, blast – I aim to live – an' spend that gold. We got Gallery – that's all that matters!'

Stephen Crane was thinking: you low-class ruffian – I can read your mind. You'd like to kill me, wouldn't you? Yes, we got Gallery in the end – and you might be next!

Eight

They rode dangerously out of the broken rocky land, urging the animals in a way that could have snapped a leg in two if the horses had put a wrong foot forward. But with the luck of their kind, the rough riders and the snorting mounts reached the sandy defile that led to the end of the rocky outcrops and then they were near to the rough corral where the pack of horses cropped at the sparse grass and Kid Dawson waited, expectant, gun at the ready.

The blonde girl was dumped in a corner among the bleached rocks and the Kid had tied a big square slab of rock to a length of rope which, in turn was looped around her wrists. She could not run far with this anchor.

'What in hell was all that shootin'?' The Kid faced them.

'We got Gallery ...'

'Dead?'

'I sighted on him,' said Stephen Crane coolly, 'and he'll be dead. Judging by the fast way he fell.' It was an arrogant comment, befitting his character and intended as a sneer at the ignorant young man.

'What was Gallery doin' here?'

'We rode right into him – and the blamed sheriff from Delta. We cut the lawman down right away ...'

'Wal, ain't that somethin'!' The Kid stood with his mouth agape, a habit he had when surprised. Then he returned to the main point. 'What in tarnation was Gallery doin' in this pile of damned rocks?'

'Must have figured it for a hideout,' said Max Kerle.

Stephen Crane rubbed his unshaven jaw. 'Now why did the sheriff visit this place? Rather strange. It isn't possible they contacted the sheriff so quickly about the loss of the gold. My, my – it doesn't really matter.'

He turned suddenly gleaming eyes to the golden-haired girl and crowded closer to her, sudden smouldering ideas burning in his brain. 'Ah, how is my dear little girl?'

When he got too close she kicked out at him and, in fact, rammed a boot against his shin. With an angry hiss of breath, Stephen Crane raised a hand as if to strike her and then thought better of it and smiled evilly. 'You'll pay for that, my dear, when I feel like dealing with you.'

'You dirty ruffian! You stinkin' inhuman brute!'

The smile vanished. 'Don't you dare talk like that to me – bitch!'

'You killed my dear father! You filth!'

The tall man just walked away, smiling grimly, but her words rankled in the mind of a man who had once commanded respect and worn the uniform of a famous regiment. He would have revenge. She would learn to respect him.

'Now, look here,' snarled Kid Dawson. 'You ain't tellin' me much. Why all that shooting? You came riding like there was Apache on your trail.'

'If we must spell it out,' sneered Crane, 'we ran into the old prospector and his daughter. I saw them – damned well pumping rifle shots at us. Seems they were friendly with Gallery. Well, they can bury him!'

That remark brought a guffaw of delight from Max Kerle. For the time being the relationship between the partners in killing was amicable.

'Are we hightailin' it to Delta with these hosses now that we've done for Gallery?'

'That's the idea,' said Kerle. 'I say we forget about any further gold in this place – for the time being. We got a lot to do.'

'We can always return.' Crane turned to them. 'At some future date, my friends. When we have had some pleasure –' And he threw another glance at Delia Breen as she hugged the rock face and glared at them. 'Perhaps by that time these simple-minded mining people will have won some more gold out of these inhospitable rocks. I have a feeling, however, that those two ruffians took all that was available.'

'Gold! We got it!' stated Kid Dawson. He grinned at the other two, his round face pudgy and slightly stupid. 'I feel good, Steve! Gallery dead – wish I'd done it – an' gold for the spendin'. Ain't it good, Max?'

He did not notice the scowl that Stephen Crane handed to him. And he certainly could not read his mind. Crane was thinking: you scruffy low-class range-rat! If you make such familiar use of my name again, I'll shoot you where you stand! You dumb young upstart!

'How about some chow?' This question from Max Kerle. 'I sure need grub. I wish I had some rotgut – or even tequila with a pinch of salt.'

'You figure the prospector and his gal will come

after us?' asked the Kid.

'Don't be stupid.' The hawklike man could not resist the dig. 'A gal and an oldster? Huh!'

'They made you ride like hell.'

'There won't be a second time. Say, let's have some blasted coffee. Light a fire, Kid. I'm sick o' drinking water ...'

Without any qualms about the killings they had left behind them, the three men busied themselves with the chores. Food was prepared, rustled from the stores belonging to the mustanger. There was soon the sizzling sound of sidemeat frying in a pan and coffee bubbling in a pot.

The girl backed to the rock-face and watched them, fearfully, because she saw the terrible truth stamped on the faces of these men. The killer stamp, knowing nothing of mercy.

'Well, if we want to reach civilization and enjoy some refined living, we've got work to do,' stated Stephen Crane. 'If we drive, we can be in Delta by nightfall – despite this heat.'

'And the hosses?'

'We'll sell them quickly. We may want to get out of town fast. Gold and money can be taken anywhere.'

'And this gal?' Kid Dawson jerked a thumb at her. 'You aim to haul her into town? She'll screech like a night-owl.'

'I won't be such a fool as to take her into a town,' countered the army man. 'I have a better idea. Just outside of Delta I've noticed an old deserted shack near the ruined mission. I'll push the girl in there until I can return – and – then –'

'Yeah?' jeered Max Kerle. He laughed sneeringly at his partner. 'This filly has sure got you goin', Crane. You figure you can handle her? Maybe you need help.'

'We share the gold – nothing else.'

The urgency of the work ahead was very real if they wanted to reach Delta by nightfall – and do some business – and so they had to get moving.

Two miles out of the town the old ruined mission stood, its crumbling walls a monument to the old *padres* who had travelled up from across the Rio Grande to found a chain of missions. But the Apache had also moved north, on frequent raids, and they wiped out the *padres* and also burnt the roof for the last time. The place had never been repaired. Some old sourdough had built a shack nearby out of the timbers salvaged, and it was to this crude shelter that Stephen Crane took the girl. He pushed her into the place, alone, the horses somewhere down the slope, near the cottonwoods, attended by Max Kerle and Kid Dawson.

'You will stay here,' said the man cruelly. 'I'll return, never fear, when I have more time. There's no need to be afraid, my girl. I am quite capable of treating you like a lady – although you are far from that status – if you will allow me to teach you.'

'I hate you!'

He laughed. 'Well, that emotion will suffice for a start. Don't you know that hate is akin to love? You don't, filly? Ah, well ...'

Her hands were still tied. He had rope and so he forced her to sit down and submit to being roped to an old rough chair. 'You will stay here – for the night. Maybe I'll come out to see you – but perhaps I'll be too drunk even to appreciate your youth.'

She had never listened to such smooth evil in her life. 'You're a monster! I swear I'll kill you!'

'How? With your bare hands?' His eyes gleamed. 'That might be an interesting scuffle because I am so much stronger than you.' He lightly touched her hair; then ran a hand down her arm. 'Ah – youth – a pity you can't come willingly to me – but perhaps in my more genial moments I might try to win you over.'

'That's impossible, you brute.'

'Just a harsh man in a harsh world,' he said grimly. 'You'll learn in the next day or two. And now I must go. My ruffianly friends insist we get to town. We need to get rid of fifty horses – quickly –'

And that was true. The pack of horseflesh, although representing a useful sum of money, was beginning to assume a nuisance value because it needed time and attention. Fifty animals had to be watched, and there were two lead mares that seemed to be imbued with an itch to wander off. Kid Dawson had cursed them repeatedly and rounded them back into the pack.

When Stephen Crane returned to the other two men, there were some snarled comments about the delay. 'Hey, when are we going to hit town and get rid of these broomtails, Crane?'

'All right – push on,' rapped the other. 'We'll find corral space to hire somewhere in the town even if we don't actually make a deal tonight. Might be better that way. We'll haggle with the army agents in our own time.'

'Wal, the blamed sheriff is dead,' joked Max Kerle. 'He can't ask nosy question now, huh? Gallery is dead, too – we don't have to worry about him. Same goes for the mustanger – he can't argue. An' them two bad hombres who so kindly lifted the gold for us – why them two galoots is plumb dead as well! Just seems like we got everything going our way, Crane, old man, Colonel, Sir!'

Stephen Crane's eyes glinted at the sheer insolence displayed by this drifter, a man he had to suffer as a partner. Kerle had better watch his tongue, he thought – and his manners. A Colt slug could even up faster than a bolt of lightning! The solid little bags of gold were a big inducement to this possible end.

The plan worked out fine for the three killers. They found a corral and the man who owned it, and agreed to pay his price for the night's hire. The pack of horses were driven through the poles and the gate made fast. As the animals swirled around the confines, Max Kerle said: 'Wal, that little chore is done. How about a drink?'

'When do we share the gold?' demanded Kid Dawson. He jigged his horse close to the other men. 'I reckon it's time …'

'We need two more canvas pokes,' said Stephen Crane smoothly.

'Why'n hell?'

'We can then share the gold out into six pokes, making two for each man. Ideally, we should weigh the stuff.'

'Rough an' ready will do for me,' grunted the Kid.

'How about getting us a room at a hotel,' suggested Max Kerle, 'an' then we can stash the gold for the night? We can sell it tomorrow. There's an assayer's office in town. They might buy it – or the bank. It's easier to share out real *dinero*.'

'You are coming up with remarkably acute ideas, Kerle.' Crane smiled sarcastically. 'I'm in favour of the hotel room and a neat hiding place for the gold until tomorrow. Then we'll sell. Dollar bills look good. We can collect on the *remuda*, too.'

'Right – share-out tomorrow,' snapped Kid Dawson. 'Maybe it's too late to sell the gold tonight ...'

'Not too late for a damned good drink!' gloated Max Kerle.

Crane looked dubious. The pleasure of drinking with these two low-class pards was not one that appealed to him. He could still recall nights in the officers' mess, with friends of some refinement – although there had been some critical times even with his kind.

They booked into a room at a cheap hotel, leaving their horses with a liveryman and tramping up the stairs of the hotel with heavy, tired limbs. It had been a long day. They needed relaxation. The gold was taken with them, along with their saddlebags and guns. It was typical of Stephen Crane that while the other two merely beat dust out of their clothes and went hurriedly to the nearest saloon, he sent for warm water. He washed, shaved and brought out a clean checked shirt from his saddlebag. When he joined the other two in the saloon, he at least looked presentable.

They had some ready cash and could buy drinks. The saloon was full of frontier characters, a card game going solidly at one table. Two white-aproned bartenders were in evidence to supply bottles and glasses. Two big girls of doubtful age and virtue were perched on the laps of two big rannigans who were clad in narrow-lapelled store suits.

'We're sitting pretty,' Max Kerle chuckled. 'Gold – and Gallery dead as all hell! Hah! Hah! Gold, eh! Gawd!'

'I hope you are not going to shout these facts from the bar-top,' said Stephen Crane coldly.

'What the hell! Crane – just cut out your goddam uppity way of talkin'. We've had a bellyful. I say we're sitting pretty – an' I don't want to listen to you tellin' me what to do.'

'You'll end up drunk.'

'Wal, ain't that great! I'd like to get drunk – you hear me! I reckon what we done deserves a few drinks – ain't that right, Kid, amigo? Ain't we done well?'

'Pretty good.' The Kid nodded foolishly. Already he had downed three shots of whisky. It was, admittedly, poor stuff and produced by some enterprising local still owner. 'Yeah, we done got rid of Gallery. Wish I'd filled him with lead. That's what I wanted – pump shot after shot into the skunk. Still –'

'We got gold!' yelled Max Kerle. 'Yes. sirree, we got enough to buy this blasted bar! Gold – heh! Heh!'

A lantern-jawed range-hand standing close to Max Kerle pricked up his ears at the mention of the word. Max Kerle gulped again at his glass and reached for the half-full bottle of golden liquid.

Stephen Crane endured another ten minutes of the fool's banter between the two men, and then decided that fools drank while other men acted. The time had arrived for him to shake off these two uncouth louts, and what better if a man rode out with more than his share of gold!

It was there, for the taking, in the hotel room, and he had the key, being the last to leave. He didn't need to get drunk. That state of idiocy could always come later.

He sidled away and made for the batwings. He went out into the night where yellow lanterns gleamed at infrequent intervals down the main stem. Some passing men tramped along the boardwalk. Further along the street, light spilled from another saloon. He heard the clanging notes of an aged piano hammered by some heavy-handed musician.

If Max Kerle and the Kid got drunk, half the men in the bar would know about the gold by midnight – and that would be dangerous.

He took big strides back down the main stem. He paused at the corral where the fifty head stood patiently. On an impulse, he lifted the retaining pole and moved into the corral. He selected a big black and a small mustang that looked obedient. He thought this horse had maybe been stolen. He led them out, holding the manes. He slid the pole back, locking the gate.

He led the two animals along to the livery and got the hostler to saddle the black with his own saddle and provide another rig for the small mustang. The two animals were brought along to the tie-rail outside the hotel. Stephen Crane went into the building, taut and grim, smiling with some inner excitement. Ten minutes later he came out with the four bags of gold, guns and his saddle-bags.

He quietly got to his saddle and, holding the lead-rope trailing to the smaller horse, he nudged the big black down the main stem.

He was leaving the fools and embarking on his own adventure, the only logical move to make in this deadly game.

Nine

They lifted him up and carried the limp body back to the cabin in the rocky gulch, a trail of blood marking their passage. Old Bert Mackay could use only one arm, and even that effort pulled muscles which gave him much pain, and he had to carry his rifle at the same time. So the bulk of the man's weight fell on Helen. She supported his shoulders and had to stop frequently. Each time they rested she noticed the eyes closed in unconsciousness – or was it near to death? This created a desperate fear in her heart. Oh, of all the futile waste!

Helen and her father had heard the gunshots soon after Jim had left with the sheriff. Fearfully, they had run out, armed. Bert Mackay had insisted upon accompanying his daughter. It was just as well that two rifles had spoken instead of one. The two men had evidently thought that caution was better than recklessness this time and had escaped down the defile.

In the house she bent over Jim. Her father brought water and a cloth which she used to bathe Jim's head. Blood had matted into his hair and painted his face fearfully like a mask. But when she wiped the blood away and cleaned him, he looked a lot better, except for the terrible long red wound right down the side of his head, just above the ear.

She slid a hand to his heart, paused, and then thrilled with a new hope.

'He isn't dead, Pa! He's alive!'

The old man nodded wisely. 'A crease! He missed death by an inch, daughter! He'll come round – maybe soon – maybe later – and he'll have a mighty sore head. And hair will never grow on that scar again.'

'He's got to live!'

'I reckon he will. He's a hard galoot, this one. Well, we'll do as much as we can for him, gal.'

But Jim Gallery stayed unconscious for a long time, concussed by the one shot that had found him. Stephen Crane had nearly accomplished his desire to murder, but not quite. His aim had been accurate, sure enough, but it seemed that Jim Gallery had moved slightly at the right split second. In a shooting match with small hand-guns – or even rifles – these things happened. This moment in time had saved a life.

She could not leave his side. She stared down at this rock-hard man who had entered her life, noted his deep breathing. Thank goodness his breathing was regular! With his eyes closed the lean face was still handsome. He had shaved earlier that day, not a common practice on the frontier, but there was still a blue shadow around his chin.

Something in his present helplessness made her stretch out a hand to lightly touch his brow. Her father, walking stiffly, entering the room at that moment, saw the gesture and smiled faintly. The way of a woman with a man to nurse!

'I'll have to get the sheriff's body back here,' muttered Bert Mackay. 'I've got to give him a decent burial. Can you help me, gal? I can't leave him out there for the pesky buzzards.'

'Those gunslingers!' Anger flushed into her face. 'Why did they have to kill Mack Slater? Who are they? Why did they come here?'

'Looks to me like they've been trailing this man, honey,' and the oldster indicated Jim Gallery.

'Why?' She paused. 'There has to be a reason ...'

'Could be anything in this hard land. We'll know pretty soon. Men make enemies, you know.'

'I hate killing!'

They went out to deal with the sheriff's body, finding this a hard, distasteful chore. But Mack Slater had always been friendly with Bert Mackay and they had to do something respectful for the body. 'I'll make a cairn, way down in the sandy draw,' said the old man. 'I won't be long, daughter.'

When Helen Mackay got back to the cabin and leaned anxiously over Jim Gallery again, she saw his eyes move, momentarily it was true, but this was a sign of returning consciousness. From then on she was in a state of excitement, watching him, leaning over him, cleaning his face again. Then she made soup, thinking he might need something reviving and nourishing.

By the time the sun was sinking way out on the rim of the badland areas, Jim Gallery was back in this world. His eyes followed the girl a bit blankly. He lay back on the bunk and when he tried to move she insisted that he lay still.

'You've been badly hurt. You must rest – Jim.'

'Wha – what happened?'

She did not burden him with a long-winded rigmarole. She simply said: 'You were creased, but you'll be all right. Just lie still. Do you like soup?'

He tried to grin but that just brought shooting

pains down one side of his face. He watched her as she busied herself around the cabin. She came with a bowl of the soup and made him swallow most of it, feeding him with a large spoon.

An hour later, when the sun had disappeared and some lone coyote howled from some lofty perch, he sat up and grinned again, despite her attempts to make him lie still. 'You're like an old hen,' he said gruffly. Then, gently, 'Thanks, Helen. It's good … to have … someone fuss a bit. But I'll be all right. I remember everything now …'

'Two men shot at you …'

'Yep. Two killers – Stephen Crane and Max Kerle.'

'Who are they? What did they want?'

'Me – mostly – dead.' He tried to laugh.

'What a grim thing to say. Why, Jim?'

'It's a kinda long story.' He pausd. 'And you wouldn't like much of it. It ain't the kind of tale a woman would appreciate.'

'Oh! But I would like to know more …'

'Wal, there's three guys – another feller name of Kid Dawson. All dangerous galoots. When you found me without boots and guns, I'd just gotten away from them. They want me dead. I left them without horses – after they'd left me to drown – It's a boring account, Helen. Sure you want to hear? One thing puzzles me – an' that's how come they rode into the Yellow Stones. How did they know I was here? Tracked? But they ain't so hot at that Injun game – I know that for sure.'

'Well, they rode away when Pa and I fired at them. They left you for dead. I bet they figure you dead.'

'They are going to get one heck of a surprise.' Jim Gallery sat up, slowly and with effort. Helen protested. 'I'm getting on my feet, young lady.

Don't try to stop me.'

'You've got a raw wound along your head.'

'It's dryin' up. I'll be fine.'

'But the shock.'

'I resist shocks like a rodeo bull.'

'You are impossible,' she gasped.

He swung his stockinged feet over the side of the bunk and sat for a few moments until his senses stopped reeling.

'You can get me my boots,' he said finally. 'Kinda strange how you always seem to see me with my boots off!'

'Where do you think you are going?'

'To Delta,' he said with the finality of a man who cannot escape some damnable sense of urgent fate. 'To see three men. That's where they'll be. Helling around – if you pardon the expression ...'

'But they might kill you, Jim Gallery!'

'No. I'll kill them!'

She stared at him fearfully. Her warm brown eyes were liquid pools of doubt and foreboding. He looked at her sideways, quizzically, the Irish heritage now deep in his facial outlines. The raw wound gave him a lopsided appearance and emphasized his grim mood. She knew he wasn't fooling. She hardly knew how to answer this disturbing, attractive man.

'Why? Why kill them? Why not just allow them to disappear?'

'They'll get around to knowing I'm not dead – one day – when I'm seen on the trails, or in some damned dusty town. Then they'll come ridin' and gunnin' for me again. Those three men want me dead, Helen. They have a burr in their minds about me – just like it is with me. They just won't rest once they know I'm alive. You see, they hate me. D'you know the kind of hate they've got?'

'I don't like to hear about hate and death.'

'I have to tell you because it's part of me -- right now, anyway. Maybe some day – when they're dead – or I'm dead – it'll be different.'

'Jim Gallery, I hate this kind of talk!'

'But you've got to know – maybe understand what kind of guy I am. They hate me for many reasons and they'll thrust through any damned danger or hardship to see me lying like a corpse because that's the only kind of answer that will give them any satisfaction. They want finality – death, in other words. Me – dead! To them brutality and death are a kind of religion. It's the only medicine they know and they aim to hand it to me. They'll do just that – when they know I'm still in this world of the rough-tough living. They'll come right after me – to corpse.'

'And you want to hand them the same treatment?' She searched his face for truths.

'I guess so – but not because of hate.' He took her hand. 'Believe this, Helen. It isn't hate. They hate – I survive.'

She moved away, restlessly. She stood at the window and looked out at the night. 'You won't be put off, I see. I'll get the horses ready.'

'Horses?'

'I'm going with you. I have friends in Delta. And someone should notify the deputy sheriff about Mack Slater.'

'Yeah. I guess that's a detail.'

'You might be too busy killing,' she pointed out grimly.

Nothing he could say would deter her. If he was obstinate, she intended to show him that she, too, could have the same streak. But there were other reasons; he might fall from his horse through a sudden weakness and she wanted to be there if anything like that happened.

He got ready slowly, drawing on reserves of deep, inner energy. He had to force himself through most of the preparations but he would not admit this to the girl. Finally, he was all set, his boots on, a Colt .45 in a holster, spare slugs in the pocket of his flapping vest and a hat on his head. He had borrowed the hat. His other one was lying somewhere in the rocks. He went out to the tie-rail where the girl had left the horses after rounding them up in the grassy, sandy hollows among the rocky sentinels.

'It'll be a slow ride to Delta,' she warned. 'It's dark – and you can't ride at full lope.'

'You're nurse-maidin' me again,' he grinned. 'Anyway, Helen, when we hit Delta you get going to your friends and I'll mosey around and see if I can get wised up.'

There was no way to defy him or argue the point. Bert Mackay stood at the tie-rail to see them off. Helen had a rifle in the saddle scabbard, and for that matter she had seen to it that Jim Gallery's mount was similarly equipped. For a girl who didn't like killing, she knew the value of guns in a tight situation. Well, it was the way of the west.

They cantered easily away from the Yellow Stones area and took to the faintly discernible trail that led to Delta. Thankfully, a glimpse of moon helped them while she watched this man closely as he sat hard in the saddle. He did not sway or show signs of faintness. He hunched grimly and, as the distance was eaten up under rapidly moving hoofs, he said little.

She tried to speak. 'What are your plans? Have you got any?'

'Just to look …'

'You mean in saloons?'

'Yep. Where else in a town like Delta and with hard cases like them three?'

'You just intend to start a fight?'

'Maybe …'

'You're not very talkative, Jim.'

'I've got a sore head, Miss Mackay, and lousy thoughts.'

'We could return – forget about those men.'

He almost snarled. 'You know that's impossible.'

She was silent after that, not wanting to annoy him. He'd had a grim time and he had a conscience – she knew that detail, no matter how many determined statements he made about life and death. She would not contribute to his tribulations, but if only he'd turn back!

Eventually, they rode into town in the moonlight, passing some street oil-lamps. The girl pointed to the light gleaming inside the sheriff's office. 'Someone there. Could be the deputy. Won't you go and see him?'

'You do it, Helen. You know who killed the sheriff – two hellions by the name of Stephen Crane and Max Kerle. The latter is wanted right through Wyoming territory. No lawman will be surprised to hear about him.'

She handed him a wary smile and left him. She couldn't change his mind, that was obvious. Such grim intent! These feelings were not emotions she could share or harbour. In this respect he was a man alone and, being a woman, she did not understand him at that moment in time. But he had left her, taking his own destiny, ready to challenge other men, perhaps ready to die.

She walked along to the sheriff's office, only twenty yards away and only a stone's throw from the house of her friend.

He didn't barge right into the first saloon. Even with his savage need to rid himself of these men, he knew it was an encounter which had to be approached slowly and with respect for the dangers.

He wished he had the makings of a cigarette. The habit was not one he indulged in very often but right now he thought the consoling tobacco might be a bit of a help. With Helen vanished into the night, he felt suddenly and unpleasantly alone, in the full stark sense of the words. Yeah, if he didn't kill them, they'd hunt him again when they discovered he was alive. That was the measure of their hate. But now, because of their ignorance of events, he had the advantage.

He was making a bet that the men were somewhere around Delta. Maybe this saloon – or maybe the next. They would want to relax in the only way they knew.

He had been around Delta often enough to know the place like the back of his hand, all the streets, banks, stores, livery stables, saloons. He knew the saloons particularly, for he was that kind of man, and a saloon was a place for men tired of sweaty horses, trail dust and warm saddles. Finally, he walked stiffly towards the first one. The sound of a tinny piano impinged on his ears as he walked.

Jim Gallery stood at the batwings and glanced warily into the place. The usual noises came to his ears, men cursing, talking, laughing. Some gent was singing a mournful ditty created by some sad man during the Civil War. Jim stared swiftly at the tables. He saw a collection of men dressed in assorted garments from buckskin to top hats, smoking cigars and having a rare night out. Some were town men and others drifters from distant ranges, and others cattle hands.

He eased warily away from the batwings. There was no sign of the three killers. He went to his horse outside; led it away down the street to where light spilled in flickering yellow beams from another saloon. He was hitching the leathers around a tie-rail when he became aware of two horses at the end of the main stem. He glanced tiredly, a mere flick of his eyes. The animals were a good three hundred yards away, moving away from him and heading out of town.

Only one horse bore a rider. The other was being led on a rope. After his first fleeting glance, Jim Gallery stiffened, hand flashing to his gun. Then he became hesitant, a rare thing in his nature.

He thought he'd seen Stephen Crane riding a big black. But the night air seemed a bit hazy at that end of the main stem. Was it a delusion? Did he have that guy on his brain? Why the horse with the empty saddle? Was it not simply some horseman of the same build? Anyway, Stephen Crane liked to ride high, wide and handsome. Cavalry-style – and not like some damned range-hand with a pack-horse.

Jim Gallery wiped sweaty hands down the sides of his pants. Grimly, he knew he was on edge. His damned head-wound was not helping. If he cased after every shadow he would make a mess of things. He thought he would stick to his original idea that the three men would be found together in some saloon. That had to be the situation. They just wouldn't have any other business at that time of night. Sure, they'd be relaxing, thinking they'd left him for dead.

He took three big strides to the batwings of the saloon, stared grimly into the smoke-haze, and like the crack of a gun two figures impacted vividly on to his brain.

Max Kerle and Kid Dawson were there, sure enough, proving his hunch. They stood with their backs to him, hunched, elbows solid on the mahogany bar and making out with talk and loud laughs. Two men, the guys he sought – but where was Crane?

And then he knew he had in fact seen Stephen Crane slowly riding down that street, disappearing into the gloom at the end of the stem. His first impression had been right. Tiredness, the wound in his head, something had affected his judgement momentarily, enough for Crane to ride away.

It was now too late to tackle the man. He had two right before him. Well, almost before him. They had their backs to him.

For some moments Jim Gallery waited, sombre, a certain tinge of grim distaste in his gut. In that second he knew he could walk away. If he did walk away, the scene would live for ever in his mind.

He began to detest the gunhawks. They were living, moving proof that all men had the killer streak in them. These guys were dragging him down to that level. Sure, he wanted them dead, because he would only survive if they were dead. Survive or die – that was the name of the game. He wished someone else would do the killing. And he was heavy with the knowledge that his first conviction was right; they'd return to hunt him the day they knew he was not dead.

Still, he waited, moving to one side as a big man pushed through the batwings, handing him a surly stare in the process.

Where was Stephen Crane going? He certainly wasn't taking the two animals to some livery because he was heading for black fringes on the rim of the town. Had these men finally argued and fallen out?

He threw another glance at Max Kerle and Kid Dawson as they shifted stance at the bar and laughed loudly. These two were pretty pally for a change! What was the good humour all about? Was it just the intoxicating drink?

Finally, almost reluctantly, thinking strangely of Helen Mackay in his fleeting thoughts, he edged into the saloon and found a space between two tables. There were no men between him and the other two rannigans.

'Kerle! Dawson!' He shouted harshly above the general din. Then again: 'Kerle! Dawson! Turn around. I want you two!'

Something in the deadly penetrating tones of his voice hit into the brains of the other two men and they turned – and froze. Jim Gallery was a ghost. He was a ghost in the shape of a man, his hand hovering above a gun, his body in the gunfighter's stance.

The tableau held for seconds – and seemed an eternity. Then, strangely, it dissolved into words, spluttering, gasping sounds from one man to another, just disbelief – but deadly guns just inches away from blasting use!

Ten

'You! Gallery! But – you're dead!' This was Max Kerle's gasping, illogical statement.

Kid Dawson added his incoherent comment. 'Crane – the liar! Allus foolin' me!'

'He looked plumb dead!' Max Kerle could only stare. 'I was there, Kid!'

Coolly, Jim Gallery had his say. 'You two rats gunned down the sheriff. I want you lot dead!'

'Figure to take us together, Gallery?' Max Kerle jeered. His brain was working swiftly now, unaffected by the drink now that danger sharpened his senses. He figured that two men could beat one. Two guns spoke twice as much death! If one man stopped a slug, it would not be Maxy, boy! He knew a trick or two – he sure did! He'd dodged through gunfights in the past. He'd survive this one. But the Kid might stop a bit of lead with his anatomy.

'I'll take you – or die!' Jim Gallery indulged in the badinage. He watched them tautly, nerves tingling into ultra-awareness. Everything else fled his mind. He saw only two men in a sharply delineated sense of the present. Nothing else mattered in this time-frozen moment. Signs gave the men away. He noted the way Kid Dawson twitched, strange in a guy with young nerves. And the grim hunch on Max Kerle's shoulders that indicated he was going to act.

Men in the saloon inched away. The card tables became round surfaces where cards ceased to move and the players sat stiffly, jaws gaping. But one man had seized on a significant fact.

'Killed the sheriff!' he echoed. 'Now who the hell says that?'

'I say it,' snapped Jim. His eyes were fixed on the two men.

'Mack Slater – dead! He was a great feller! Them murdering skunks done it, you say?'

'I say it.'

The man muttered angrily, turned to the others. 'Mack Slater's dead. Now ain't that real bad! He was a friend – a real good hombre.'

'Real good hombres die just the same as other men,' snapped Jim Gallery. 'Especially when there's hellions like these around. They killed the sheriff – along with another gunny.'

The word-play held. 'Crane!' muttered Kid Dawson. 'Where the hell is Crane?'

'Lighting out, I think,' said Jim Gallery. 'I've just seen him – leading another hoss – saddled.'

'The gold!' cursed Max Kerle in a great roar. 'Hell, that swine has the gold! I bet. Sure. What else! Gawd, we've been fooled!'

'What damned gold are you yapping about, Kerle?'

'The gold we lifted from two galoots way back on the trail,' sneered Kerle. 'Yeah, we struck it rich, Gallery – and I'm gonna live to spend it. I'll get Crane …'

'Gold? You mean four small pokes?'

'We do – iffen it's any business of yours, Gallery.'

'The girl and her pa at Yellow Stones had gold stolen from them.'

'Sure – an' we lifted it from the two jiggers that rode out with it. And we got a pack of horses – after you left us to walk – bastard!'

'And now Stephen Crane has gone off with the lot,' mocked Jim Gallery. 'Ain't that somethin'?'

Max Kerle could stand the situation no longer. Words were not his tools. The compulsion to act was so strong, he clawed for his gun in a frenzy of fury. He was raging not only at Jim Gallery but at being tricked by Stephen Crane, the smooth rogue with the fancy talk. He had a vivid impression of the man riding away, laughing, making sneering remarks about fools and their gold being easily parted. That swine – carrying all the gold that meant so much!

Max Kerle was boiling with fury but, strangely, that did not affect his judgement and the plan he hoped to put over.

Kid Dawson dived a clawing hand for his gun. Two hands rammed down out of sheer habit but one went to an empty holster. He was wishing he had his twin guns, the ones he had been so fast with. But wishing is not fact. And Kid Dawson learnt that lesson the hard way.

As Max Kerle hauled his sixgun from his scuffed leather holster, he dived with astonishing speed to the right, firing swiftly. He had time to trigger off two shots.

Kid Dawson fired wildly as his Colt whipped up. The explosion coincided as he staggered forward blindly, a red hole appearing in his forehead and he fell, his life force shattered.

The shots from Max Kerle's gun hissed over Jim Gallery's head, proving that even an expert man can be too hasty. The hawklike man had intended to blast Jim Gallery between the eyes but, in diving, his gun had angled slightly.

Jim felt the slugs cut thin air above his head and he flinched. Kid Dawson's solitary shot was affected by the way his body jerked under the impact of the death-dealing slug and his bullet flew to the saloon ceiling. Then the Kid crumpled. In moments he was a dirty heap, looking oddly small in his range gear, the blood already oozing from the hole in his head and smearing his face.

In diving to the right, Max Kerle avoided the shot that Jim Gallery blasted at him by a fraction of an inch – and then the cunning range-rider rammed into a table, upsetting it. The heavy lump of pine thudded on to its side, providing a thick shield for the man.

Jim Gallery hunched and triggered off another shot. This bit deep into the table and stayed there. Max Kerle whipped off a chance shot, poking out his head and a hand momentarily. Jim fired at him but again the man dodged death by a split second. And Max Kerle's fast shot was obviously wide – but it scattered the remaining men in the saloon like frightened chickens in a farmyard!

Max Kerle knew he had to keep moving or die. He reached out, grabbed a chair leg and hurled the thing right over the table and into Jim Gallery. As Jim staggered, ducking involuntarily, Max Kerle rushed to the door at the side of the saloon. Right there and then, in his seething mind, was only one thought – apart from living to tell the tale – and that was to get away and hunt down Stephen

Crane, the smooth hateful bastard! Sudden blazing hatred of the man overcame even his dislike of Gallery.

The flying chair halted Jim sufficiently – as he dodged it – to allow Max Kerle to grab at the door handle and wrench the thing open. As he darted into the black night, another shot from Jim's Colt blasted after him and chipped wood splinters from the wall where Kerle's head had been only a second previously.

And then Kerle was escaping into the night, darting behind a building, moving with the speed of a mountain cat in his rage. When Jim Gallery got to the same door and stared out, the man had gone, vanished into the night. Jim cursed, not knowing which way to go, right or left.

He was about to leap out of the doorway when a man behind him touched his arm. Jim wheeled, gun in hand, mouthing protests. 'Say, stranger, you could get yourself killed!'

He saw a solid-looking man who obviously had something to say. 'Them gents rode into town with a pack of horseflesh – fifty head I'd say. They've got them in the old corral ...'

'Fifty hosses! Where the hell did they get them?'

'I dunno ... they told the corral owner they figured to sell 'em tomorrow.'

'Did you see the three men in here – the saloon, I mean?'

'Sure thing. One went out not so long ago – the tall galoot with the greying hair ...'

'Stephen Crane. I saw him.' Jim Gallery was talking to himself.

'Them gents booked in at the Star Hotel – I was told – by the corral owner –'

The Star Hotel! Jim Gallery knew the place. The hunch hit him powerfully that Max Kerle would have his horse stabled for the night not too far from the same hotel. And Kerle would need a mount.

Jim Gallery rushed out of the saloon. If the deputy was around he could sort out the facts behind Kid Dawson's death, and maybe Helen Mackay could help in that direction. He leaped on to the saddle of his horse, but before he could rowel the animal forward a man rushed in front of him and grabbed the headstall. 'Hey! You said the sheriff was dead! Mack Slater dead?'

'That's right. They killed him. Let go that harness, mister …'

'Now, look, I was a pal of Mack Slater. How come he got killed?'

'He was just gunned down. Quit hangin' on to that leather, partner, I want to go.'

'That corpse in there one of the killers?'

'He was one of three …'

Jim Gallery nudged his horse and the man had to stop detaining him. But time had been wasted. He set the animal into a full lope down the street and then hauled it up on haunches before the cheap hotel. Then he decided Max Kerle could be at the livery.

It was obvious that Kerle knew where Stephen Crane was heading. The man had the gold, the sacks that had been stolen from Helen Mackay and her father. So they had intercepted the two robbers who had originally lifted the valuable pokes of gold nuggets. It wasn't difficult to guess at the fate of those two men: more victims of the killer stamp! They would be dead, full of lead slugs. And they had taken horses from the men. It all added up in character for Crane and his cronies, but where did the pack of fifty animals fit in?

'Who the devil did they rob to get them?' mused Jim grimly.

That problem hardly mattered for the moment. So Stephen Crane had lit out with the stolen gold, finally double-crossing his two pards – one now dead! Well, that figured. It was in character. Gold had distorted the minds of better men than Stephen Crane in the past. Greed for gold! It was nothing new.

With all the tension of the past events crowding him, Jim Gallery felt a throbbing in his head. It seemed the raw wound was protesting. Could he go on at this pace?

Well, he felt he had to get going, push on to his destiny. Where was Max Kerle? Was he in the livery or at the hotel, grabbing at his gear? He knew he just had to push after this man.

Finally Jim figured that the man would be at the livery. These were only seconds of fleeting thought – and then all at once the rapid thud of hoofs indicated a rider thrusting a mount to full gallop. A dark shape, crouched low on the saddle, raced around the block and tore into the dark night air. Kerle!

Jim nudged his animal into instant chase and he hauled out his handgun. He pumped off two shots at the shadowy target and then realized the gun was empty when it clicked futilely. He thrust it back to leather, cursing his carelessness.

But it soon became obvious that Max Kerle was not riding the mount that had taken him into Delta, for the horse was strong and fresh, full of sinewy zest. The pounding hoofs soon took the man swiftly along the outgoing trail. A stand of cottonwoods loomed up like black shadows in the night and Jim Gallery could barely see the rider and horse ahead. Kerle had grabbed at some saddled mount in the livery, a good horse, some man's proud product of training and breeding. In that gunslinger's catalogue of crimes horse-stealing was the least heinous.

He seemed to have some destination in mind. Jim's hunch became stronger. Max Kerle knew where to find Stephen Crane – and the tantalizing gold! That must be the answer.

That precious metal, so hardly won, belonged to Helen Mackay and her father. So he'd be damned if he'd let these rats take it! In any case there would surely be a rumpus if and when Max Kerle caught up with Stephen Crane. Some gink might end up dead! Now which one? That was an interesting conjecture!

Jim Gallery muttered grimly as he peered ahead, seeing only odd glimpses of the swiftly moving rider whose horse was pounding the hell out of the trail. His own animal was tired and not in the same class as the mount Kerle had grabbed. Maybe the man might lose him.

For a moment he considered taking a chance number of shots at Max Kerle, using the rifle in the saddle scabbard, but it was very dicey because the man was drawing well ahead.

And maybe that was not the best plan. Maybe if he allowed Kerle to locate Stephen Crane, the two could kill each other – and maybe not. But this might lead to the recovery of the gold that belonged to Helen and her father. And that was a darned sight more important than cadavers!

The Killer Stamp

So for the time being it was a chase and an uncertain one at that. The other man was well ahead, somewhere out there on the shadowy trail, and Jim's horse was tiring. The unequal race could not last much longer because Max Kerle would draw so far ahead that keeping track of him would be impossible. The man had a very good horse.

Grimly, tiredly, his head throbbing again, he felt his old mixture of hatred and disgust for these men. One was dead. Was it two to go? The gold belonged to Helen. This was a new intent in his life. He'd see that the girl and her father retrieved the gold for which they had worked so hard.

And then what? Would he seek out Harry Carslake and the missing loot from the Drago Cattlemen's Bank? Or was he becoming sick and tired of it all?

He hardly knew what prompted these thoughts but there was this mental vision of Helen and the disapproval there would be in her brown eyes if he told her the truth about himself. He'd been lawless. He had been a gunhand, but he had only killed when challenged and in self-defence. Somewhere, deep inside him, he felt that the lawless frontier life was fading out as a way of living for him, and he realized that Helen had hardened his thoughts in that direction.

These ideas, momentary, fleeting, taking little time to flash through a tired mind, dispersed again when he thought he saw a dark shape of rider and horse leave the trail and, with long leaps of haunches and forelegs, climb the steeply rising ground to the right.

This was Max Kerle, he was sure, moving off the trail. A stand of old oaks blurred into a mass of darkness and swallowed the other rider. Where was he going?

Well, he just had to follow, trusting to luck. He had a feeling they were only about two miles out of town, but it had been a fast ride, a confused one in the darkness. His horse was tuckered out, nostrils flaring, eyes gleaming wildly. He sympathized with the crittur, as any range-hand would, feeling affinity with another living creature.

He got another glimpse of the rider ahead when his horse breasted a rise and he was momentarily a dark shape against a slightly lighter shade of gloom, and then he was gone. But the sighting was enough for Jim Gallery. He urged his animal into another snorting gallop. Hoofs dug at earth. The night air felt cool.

Max Kerle pressed on towards the old ruined adobe walls of the mission just ahead, and there was the shack, a light glinting thinly from the one window. Crane was there!

He'd gotten a good start — and he was there with the gold and the damned girl on whom he had fixed his lecherous eyes. Of all this there was no doubt. Whether Crane knew he would be followed was a matter for conjecture. The hard-case must have known there was the possibility that he would be followed.

Max Kerle cursed the pursuer behind him. Without the nuisance of Jim Gallery he could have dealt with Stephen Crane in his own good time. There was only one way to deal with a skunk. He would like to de-gut the man! Back shooting was too good for him. A knife in the ribs or guts was one way to get revenge on a sarcastic swine who had needled him for so long. The knife was the really gory way to handle Crane. A man could stab repeatedly, savouring the full flavour of punishment.

He had a knife. But maybe he'd be forced to use a gun. He would see how the dirty devil turned.

But Jim Gallery was a troublesome, tricky factor in this set up. Could he handle him first and then deal with Crane?

Max Kerle raced his animal past the gloomy walls of the old mission and then drew the mount up in a swirl of hoof-dust. What better place to ambush the following man! Sure, he would kill Jim Gallery first and then spring an attack on Crane and finally secure the gold.

Once again he thought about the marvellous silence of the knife. If he could get Jim Gallery with the blade, Crane would not be alarmed. If Crane wasn't warned by some shooting, he could creep up on the rat. And that would be the final killing, all the others salivated!

On drawing his horse to a halt, Max Kerle wheeled the animal around and nudged the horseflesh into the shelter of the old adobe walls. He leaped down. He didn't bother to hitch the animal. There wasn't time. He raced to the nearest corner and peered out, listening. He heard the approaching sound of Gallery's animal: hoofs drumming, a snort from an obviously tired crittur. Delighted, he judged the other rider would race up on a line almost abreast of the old adobe wall.

Max Kerle drew his Bowie knife from the sheath that had been sewn into the gunbelt long ago. It had been a long time since he had used the knife.

But there was no time for vengeful thought, no

matter how fleeting. The rider he hated was fast approaching ...

As Jim Gallery's mount stretched protesting legs in the last few yards to the shack, where the light proved there was someone inside, Max Kerle leaped out at rider and horse.

The animal whinnied in sudden fear, jerking madly. The black shape, hurtling with all the ferocity of a striking mountain cat, scared the horse. Jim Gallery was warned with only a splintered second in which to react.

And then Max Kerle's arms were around his waist and he was tugged from the saddle and the horse reared, came feet down again and as Jim left the saddle leather the animal cantered in fright. The night air swallowed the cayuse.

As Jim Gallery thudded to earth he saw the sudden gleam in the scant light of the night and knew this for a wicked knife. He rolled desperately, bringing the other man over with him.

The Bowie stabbed into the earth and Jim Gallery knew what he was up against. He recalled Max Kerle's affection for the Bowie knife. Sure the guy had other good reasons for using a knife – silence.

And Jim Gallery's own Colt was at the moment useless. The chamber was empty!

Eleven

Stephen Crane reached the shack beside the old ruined mission and slid down slowly from saddle leather, tying the two horses to the remains of an ancient tie-rail. He took time off to stare around. His lurid mind was full of anticipation.

He had the key to the battered but thick old door. This key had been fashioned by some blacksmith and was about seven inches long. He had found it inside the shack when he had left, and so he had tried the lock and found it still turned.

He hoped Max Kerle and Kid Dawson were bent upon getting really drunk back in town. That would surely keep them occupied.

He opened the door and walked into the cabin. He did not bother to lock the door this time but stared in admiration and some delight at the bound figure of the fair-haired girl. He had left the lamp burning low – because he was, after all, a gentleman – and she had apparently been struggling with her bonds. Her face was flushed; her eyes furious when she saw his approach. Two buttons on the checked shirt had split away with her struggles, and her womanly shape was something his lecherous eyes noted at once.

'Well, my dear, I'm back. To give you some

comfort, no less. You didn't imagine I'd leave you here for ever, did you?' His mocking tones were as false as his pretences.

'Go away, you killer.'

He stood over her; eyed her so deliberately, his gaze travelling over her body with such evil intent, that she paled in fear. Her head flinched back as if to get away from him, but the rope held her otherwise.

'You and I are going to take a little journey.' He placed a tentative hand on her shoulder; gripped hard when he felt the soft flesh underneath the shirt. There was something so ominous in his very touch. How she wished she could run away – but that was impossible.

She gave a little sob. 'I hate you! I hope you die! Someone will kill you!' It was a verbal thrust that made him compress his lips. 'Beast!' she flung at him. 'Murderer!'

Even the callous nature of this man disliked the pure hate which poured from her. He tried to smile. 'You'll soon get used to me, my dear. You're a woman – although devastatingly youthful – and I have a way with women. You will not hate me for long. You see, we shall travel together – share everything – and it is in the nature of a woman to submit. I know you will accept me. Well, we have to move – so I will undo these ropes. Don't try to escape ...'

He began work on the bindings that tied her to the rickety old chair but he did not loosen the ropes on her wrists. As he worked, his cold eyes stared broodingly at the soft contours of her breasts, so much that she shuddered and sobbed again.

He tried an almost foolish attempt at gallantry.

'You know, I was an officer in a fine regiment – drank only the best wines in India and was attended by native servants. I had my own batman – splendid fellow. I was following a great career until – until – well, that hardly matters now. I mention this, you lovely young thing, to show you that you have nothing to fear – if you only do as I say!'

Her answer was swift and earthy. 'You're a swine and a rogue, that's all! Like my pa would say – a no-account drifter!' And now that she was free to struggle, she hit out at him with her fists bound together.

The retaliation enraged Stephen Crane and knocked a hole in his attempt at dignity. Her lithe young arms swung her bound fists and hammered into his face. She was like a wild creature turning on an attacker.

He gave a snarl of anger that swept away his pretence and then he deliberately hit her. It was a hard blow to the chin that would have hurt any man. She sank dazedly to the ground, her corn-coloured head lowered.

'Damn you! Of all the she-cats! I think a thrashing with a belt is the medicine to teach you humility. Yes, that will also give me some pleasure.'

He unbuckled the two-inch wide leather belt which encircled him and flailed it. His gunbelt sagged on his waist.

'You asked for it, my dear – the first lesson!' His features were twisted in a leer. 'Just a taste of the belt! Ah, the humility the belt imposes! But we haven't much time, more's the pity, because there are gun-happy men who must know where to find me. We have to move on. Well, I have good horses ...'

He cracked the belt again. The girl screamed: 'Aagghh –'

The little man crouched in half-witted fear in a corner made by two crumbling walls of the old mission, and he watched the ferocious fight that ensued between the two men in a sort of scared fascination. His steeple-shaped hat, ragged, full of holes, was pulled down almost to his eyebrows and his blanket was wrapped tightly around him. Mungo Casson knew how to huddle in any corner for a night. It was his way of living.

He had actually been living inside the old walls for some weeks, without benefit of a roof, and making a weekly trip to Delta on foot, because he owned nothing. In town he scrounged for anything that was useful to a bum who had no intelligence or inclination for work.

The fight on the open ground just outside the old mission scared him to hell. But he watched, like some creature of the night seeing a struggle between giants. And Mungo was afraid. Men who fought might easily turn on him – if he revealed himself!

And how they fought! Two men rolling over and over on the earth! The sounds of their scuffle came harshly to his ears, frightening a little man who was timid in any case. They rammed fists at each other. Something gleamed momentarily. A knife! He knew all about knives. He'd been cut before. These men would kill. He, Mungo Casson, would let them kill each other while he hugged his comforting corner. Maybe he was like a mouse but he did not want to kill or be killed.

As for Jim Gallery it really seemed like a fight to

the death. For one thing, the wound on his head opened and began to throb again. And Max Kerle seemed possessed by all the fury of the devil. No doubt the rannigan was crazed with anger against Stephen Crane. The man had the gold.

Jim Gallery had seen the light in the shack; guessed that Crane had made for this place. Why, he wasn't sure. Did the man think it a hideout for the night? Why make for this place in the way he had? And Max Kerle had known exactly where to find Crane. Strange ... but right now he had a fight on his hands.

He held the man's knife at bay, using all the strength in his hands and arms, grimacing with the effort. The throbbing in his head seemed to warn him that his strength was not unlimited.

Kerle glared down at him, his face a mask in the faint light. He jerked sideways, loosening Jim Gallery's grip on his knife hand. Kerle slashed down again – and Jim rolled, but only a few inches because Kerle was on top of him, using his weight to pin him down.

The knife sliced past Jim's ear and made a cut in the earth. Kerle jerked it free again. As it moved Jim Gallery punched at the guy's face. His fist connected, a desperate blow that had all his energy behind it. Max Kerle gasped like a hog kicked in the belly. But the knife was still in his grip. A man could stand a number of blows but a knife-wound could be final. Jim Gallery knew he just had to get that weapon out of the man's fist.

He brought up a boot and kicked at the other man, ramming it into the crotch. This was a vengeful, vicious blow and caught Kerle unawares. The man was concentrating all his efforts on using the knife. The pain caused by the boot made him howl and slowed his desperate efforts to kill or maim. Jim thrust the man back with two bunched fists and then scrambled to his feet. He felt better on his feet.

He came at Max Kerle again, determined to end the fight and he knew he'd use any means in his power. If his gun had been loaded, he'd have shot the guy where he lay. But the weapon was empty and there just was not an opportunity for re-loading. But he could use it as a club.

Swinging the gun, the butt-end hacking through the air, he came at Max Kerle as the man scrambled to his feet. Jim lunged with the gun-butt and missed anything solid. Kerle had leaped back. Then the other man came in again, his knife upraised, the ugly look on his face indicating that he wanted to kill and finish his enemy.

As the knife thrust at his throat, Jim Gallery swayed back and missed the vicious blade by the thickness of a playing card. Then quick as a flash, with hellish strength surging through him, his gun-butt hacked down and connected with Max Kerle's cranium. The man sank.

Even as his knees buckled, Jim Gallery rushed in again and grabbed at the almost limp knife hand. He twisted the blade from the guy's grip and flung it far into the night. At that moment Max Kerle sagged to the ground, unconscious for the moment.

Jim looked down savagely at the beaten man. He wished him dead. But this desperado would revive unless ...

After pausing to gulp in fresh air, Jim began to load his Colt. Slowly he inserted the bullets and

The Killer Stamp   121

then paused again. The gun ready, he pointed it at the prone man. And then he hesitated.

For a crazy moment he wondered just who he thought he was to mete out this kind of justice. He had a fanciful vision of Helen Mackay somewhere in the gloom. This was a delusion and he hardly knew why this picture of the girl was in his mind, but it was enough to deter him. His gun lowered. Breathing hard, almost rasping in his throat, he wondered why he did not finish off this rat of a man.

He knew that Kerle was wanted for murder in Wyoming, and possibly elsewhere. And he was a party to the killing of the sheriff. The law could hang him – some day.

Jim Gallery sucked in fresh air and groaned. He knew in that strange moment that he was sick and tired of the law of the individual gun. He had no legal right to kill even a brute like Kerle in cold blood. Maybe in self-defence – but that was all.

He holstered his gun; turned away.

There was still Stephen Crane and the gold. If the man was inside that shack, the gold would be with him. And Crane was another human rat who had little right to anything.

Jim Gallery bent over the unconscious Max Kerle and took off the man's bandanna and then, rolling him over, he tied his hands behind his back with the neckerchief. Then Jim took his own bandanna and used it to bind Kerle's ankles together. That would immobilize the range-rat until he could be handed over to the law and a trial.

Jim straightened. He stared at the shack, which lay not so far away. He then carried Max Kerle into a corner of the old walled mission courtyard and dumped the heavy man. The ruffian could be found again later. Even as he dropped the carcass, he heard the man groan. So he was coming round! Well, he wouldn't escape those bonds in a hurry!

Jim Gallery went to look for his cayuse. He found two animals; there was Kerle's mount, nibbling at some tufts of grass, and his own horse wasn't too far away.

He held his own horse by the leathers and decided to stick with it. The other animal had an owner somewhere. The horse he held had originally belonged to Kid Dawson, not that he would be objecting!

Jim Gallery walked slowly and grimly towards the shack. He knew he had to concentrate his wits on this new problem. Why, for instance, was Stephen Crane in this place?

Even as Jim Gallery disappeared into the night, moving to the shack and the problem of Stephen Crane and the gold, a little man crawled out of a corner of the mission walls like some rodent seeking food.

Little Mungo, with his brains addled by years of sun and lonely living, was curious, now that the fight had ceased. He could see pretty well in the dark, strangely enough, like some creature who habitually moved in gloom, and he knew there was a bundle in a corner of the courtyard. This heap looked dead. Mungo knew about death. He had seen it first-hand. Dead folk didn't hurt a guy. The other big man had left him for dead. Wal, there were always pickings on the dead – for a man who didn't mind poking and prodding!

Mungo Casson pulled his blanket tightly around him and scuttled over, warily, for he was a timid man. He crouched over the bound body and blinked. Then the dead man gave a groan and Mungo nearly ran away. But, unusually brave, he stayed and listened.

The man made rasping noises deep in his throat, opened his eyes and glared at the strange little shape before him. The man struggled against his bonds, something that scared Mungo a bit. Mungo did not like anything violent. Then: 'Who – the hell – are you?' the rasping voice demanded.

'Mungo – just Mungo!' The little bum got ready to run away. Then he added with a peculiar pride: 'I live here …'

'Yeah?' Max Kerle struggled up and Mungo backed. Kerle realized he was bound at the same time that recollections of the fight between him and Jim Gallery flooded back. So the damned hell-bent had beaten him! Bound him – the hell!

Kerle stared at the little hunched shape in the blanket. 'Hey – you untie – these blamed kerchiefs! C'mon …'

'I can't!'

'You what?'

'You'll hit me! Mungo don't like bein' hit …'

Max Kerle suppressed an urge to curse the odd little galoot. 'Get me outa this. I'll give you money …'

'Dollars?'

'Anything you want, feller. C'mon – just help me get free.'

'I dunno … Mungo scared!'

'Look, I got money – you know – *dinero!* Now just untie these blamed kerchiefs. You can do it. I won't hurt you – that's a promise.'

But the odd little man with a fear of everything

moving took a lot of convincing. Kerle tried not to glare. The darkness helped him and Mungo began to nod as Kerle talked with persuasion. But all the same valuable time passed because the little guy could not be hurried.

Twelve

Jim Gallery slowly approached the rough old shack, leading his horse, his eyes fixed grimly on the low yellow light behind the solitary window. As he came up, he saw the two horses hitched outside the place. One was the smaller saddled animal he was sure he had seen Stephen Crane leading away at the darkened end of the main street in Delta. Now why did the man want a second horse? A trailing cayuse always slowed a man.

The need for caution was so obvious that Jim halted and left his horse standing. The animal just stood, tired, head drooping. He felt his usual sympathy for any cayuse he rode. The horse was sometimes a man's best pal, even more than a rifle.

But a tired crittur wouldn't stray. So he could just move on, feet as silent as possible on rough ground. No soft turf here.

He checked his gun. Loaded. Ready to kill again? The thought seemed ugly and he didn't know why. He compressed his lips, fatigue tugging at his guts. He figured he would use the gun in self-defence only – surely! The old premise of hunting Kerle and Crane because they would hunt him seemed to have ebbed from him. He wished he could explain to Helen Mackay, but she was in Delta and she still thought he was seeking vengeance.

He was, in a sense. He intended to see that the gold went to the rightful owners. They had worked hard for it. It irked him that rogues could just take everything.

He stood in the night air, his wits sharpened to the oddities of this situation because there was something strange about Stephen Crane's presence in this rough shack. Why did he require two horses?

That the man had the gold there was little doubt, but why he should make for this shack seemed a mystery. And Kerle had known exactly where to find him. Surely if Crane had wanted to lose himself in the night he would not have gone to a place where he knew another man could locate him! So he had a reason for visiting this shack. Could it be some small detail – guns – food – maybe a map?

While Jim Gallery was musing grimly on the probabilities, the gun in his hand, a scream tore out of the old shack like the cry of someone in agony! Surprised, Jim realized the sound came from a woman's throat. A woman in there – with Crane!

There was inevitably a moment when he froze and thought swiftly over the facts. What the hell had Crane gotten into? A woman! He had heard tales before about Crane's strange tastes in women. Was this the reason why Crane had travelled to this shack and not hightailed it for the open range or some town where he could hide? Had the man lost his reason? Gold – and now a woman! What kind of woman? What sort of damned rendezvous was this?

He walked forward, his Colt poking out like a

grim symbol of justice. He'd use it, swiftly, if need be in spite of his previous doubts and uncertainties.

He reached the shack door and noticed it was slightly ajar. At that moment another frightened scream tore out from inside the cabin. Then he heard a girl's voice. 'Don't – please! Don't! Ah!'

There was a sound like a whip – or leather slapping hard against something – and the girl's cry came again. Then he heard Crane's snarled advice. 'Shut up! You young idiot – I'm merely teaching you a lesson. There's no need to waken the dead, damn you. Some bitches actually like this sort of thing!'

Jim Gallery rammed the door back as if he would crash it off the hinges. At the same time, in one swift motion, his legs took him into the cabin. One glance was enough.

'Drop that belt, Crane – or by heaven I'll puncture your gut!'

The big man turned in surprise, the belt hanging limply, his cold eyes glinting when he saw Jim Gallery. 'You! My God – you should be dead!'

The girl stared in doubt, but only for seconds, fear and shock still on her face. She ran to a corner of the shack as some sort of reaction. Her hands were bound, Jim Gallery noted grimly, but her feet were free. She shouted: 'Help me – please – help me!'

'Drop that belt, Crane,' Jim angrily flung the direction at the man. 'Hell, so it's true what they say about you and women!'

Jim's Colt poked forward like some menacing metallic machine ready for bloody reprisal. Stephen Crane swayed in doubt as if he was unable to believe that Jim existed. But the threatening Colt was real. Crane knew that Gallery was a dangerous man if he had reason to act. Crane suddenly dropped the belt. Then even in this situation he had to resort to words.

'You were dead – I was sure – how the hell did you get here?'

'You answer the questions, you gentlemanly dirt! Who is this girl? I won't even ask you what you're doin' to her.'

'She's just some young bitch –'

'I'm Delia Breen,' cried the girl. 'Help me! My father was the mustanger – they stole our horses – killed my poor pa –'

'Ah, the fifty head of horses.' Jim nodded. 'I wondered how they fitted in.'

'We were on the trail to Delta and these filthy men rode down on us and just shot my pa in cold blood ...'

'That figures. What else?'

'They made me go with them – tied – to a place called Yellow Stones. And then after some fight in the hills they came back – drove the pack of horses to Delta. Oh, God – get me away from this mad, murdering skunk!'

'You're going to be all right. You don't need to tell me much more. I can figure it all out.' Jim swung to Stephen Crane. 'Seein' we're doin' a lot of talking, you might as well know that Kid Dawson is dead and Kerle was all set to gun for you.'

'Kerle? Where is he?'

'As it happens, outside – in the dark – hogtied. I'm handing him over to the law.'

Stephen Crane laughed and relaxed. His body eased from the tense attitude he had taken; his right hand hovered just above his gun-butt. It was something that Jim Gallery noted with a grim expression.

'You know, Jim, old man, you and I could do a neat little deal. Unless you want to court death.'

'Go on, mister ...'

'Gold is a fascinating substance, don't you agree? Men fight and die for it. Now we don't have to reach that desperate level; as gentlemen, we can share this valuable metal and ride out as partners.'

'All right, pal ...'

'You agree?' Stephen Crane was surprised and suspicious, his lips curling in a sneer.

'Yeah. Just drop your gunbelt – slowly –'

The big man with the cunning mind saw the trick coming up. 'That isn't a deal, Gallery. You just want to disarm me.'

'It was worth a try ...'

Both men stared for some seconds. The girl was a fascinated observer. Crane's hand twitched fractionally closer to the gun lying snugly in his shiny holster. 'You'll have to do better than that, Gallery. Let's talk it over – as gentlemen –'

'I'm no gent – and you are something that crawled out of a hog's dung!'

'Put that gun of yours in leather and insult me again – and draw for it.' Crane's fury was slowly rising. His face was a pale mask. 'Just give me a chance – as man to man –'

'You never gave any galoot a fightin' chance in your life,' snapped Jim Gallery. 'But all right – you can go for your iron when you like.'

And the lean tired man with the wary scowl on his Irish face shoved his Colt into the holster. He waited, watching Crane and the twitches on his visage. When would the man draw? And who was the quickest with a hogleg?

Crane waited, his brain racing, scheming. 'Gold, you idiot! Don't you like gold, Mister Gallery? Don't you realize it's a fair amount of loot shared just two ways? Damn, you bucked the law for less than that! Are you trying to adopt a halo in your latter days? What's wrong with you, Gallery? Don't you like money – wealth?'

'It's all there – outside – ain't it?' Jim said with a strange smile. 'I could start shootin' an' kill you – and then ride off with the gold.'

'I might kill you. In fact, I will. I'm pretty fast, Gallery …'

'You might,' Jim nodded.

'Look, I'll allow the girl to go free.' Crane licked dry lips and Jim noticed the little nervous action.

'You will?'

'She's nothing to me – just a diversion.'

'You've been giving her hell, you swine – with that belt.'

'She's just a bitch! You understand, Gallery! Women – what are they to men like us?'

Jim Gallery thought fleetingly of Helen Mackay. 'Are you ready, Crane?'

'She can go, damn it! All I want is gold! Have we an agreement, Gallery?'

'No. When you're ready, Crane.' Jim Gallery's eyes flinted in the faint yellow light. The girl was in her corner, staring in fascination, speechless for the moment, sensing the hate and the remorseless inner pressures of these two men. 'Go for that iron just any time you like.'

A silence fell that seemed to last for a horrifying time, and then with a speed that was starkly paralysing to the girl the two men clawed for guns.

The Killer Stamp

Crack! Crack!

The two shots exploded inside the shack like cannons in a battle. Both men had hunched. Both men held smoking guns. They stared for a long time – but maybe it was only seconds.

Stephen Crane smiled strangely. Jim Gallery watched him, frozen in his last attitude.

Stephen Crane slowly lost his smile as his gun sank. Red blood had time to soak into his shirt as his heart pumped on in the last few seconds of life, and then he fell slowly sideways – and forwards – and hit the wood planks of the cabin floor.

The girl shrieked again and again as the echoes died away and the odour of gunsmoke swirled around the shack. Jim sank his Colt into leather and took long strides over to her and placed a comforting arm around her shoulders. Then he stared grimly at Crane, now an awful heap on the floor. Crane's shot had missed Jim by a hair's breadth, his gun hand jerking as Jim's faster shot hit into his flesh.

'You'll be all right, gal! Don't be too afraid. He had it coming ...' Jim thought fleetingly of Helen and found it easy to console the girl.

'Oh, please get me out of here! Oh, I wish I could see my pa!'

'But he's dead ...'

'Oh, I know. God, I'm so confused! That man – he wanted to beat me – he –'

'Just try to forget. You'll get to Delta. There's a horse outside this shack. Go to the sheriff's office and ask for the deputy. Then ask for a girl called Helen Mackay. Tell her everything.'

'I don't want to ride alone ...'

'Wal, it's only a few miles ...'

'I want you to go with me.'

Jim Gallery smiled gently. 'You trust me – after this man?'

'I can trust you – I know. I'll ride back with you to Delta.'

'All right,' said the lean, tired man. 'Fine. But I've got some little chores, gal. This body will have to be tied over a horse. And then there's a hellion outside who'll need fixin' to another cayuse. All little chores but we'll get them done – an' then ride for town. Maybe this is the end of the line. It is for this so-called gent – Stephen Crane.'

'You're feeling low, aren't you?' murmured the girl.

'Yeah – strange – guess I'm doggone tired. As for Crane, I can't even damn his soul even in death because he never had one. And there's another hell-bent outside I've got to deal with …'

'I'll help you,' said the girl. 'I'm pretty hard, you know. I used to help pa with a pack of half-wild horses – an' that ain't so easy …'

Jim Gallery smiled faintly.

But right at that moment Max Kerle was free. The odd little man, Mungo Casson, in his foolishness, had untied the range crook. Then Kerle had sent him running in wild terror with a vicious blow. The little bum had served a purpose.

Eyes glinting with a smouldering rage against a guy called Jim Gallery, Kerle knew he still had a chance. He could kill his enemy and enrich himself at the same time. The gold was there. But he was weaponless. Gallery, blast him, had thrown the knife away and taken his gun, too, probably disposing of it. But there would be guns for a man who had surprise on his side.

As he stood up, churning over his raging thoughts, wishing he could strangle Gallery with his bare hands, such was his hate, he heard the sharp report of two gunshots.

Jerking his head, he knew they had come from the cabin. Now who had killed whom? Or were both dead? God, that was maybe too much to ask the devil for!

With his arms hanging limply by his sides, his fists balled in anger, he lurched forward. His head ached from the blow he had gotten from Jim Gallery's gun-butt. Even as he moved on, dirt and sweat caked on his face, he knew there was a need for caution. But even so he was impelled by sheer hate to go after Gallery. He hated the tall lean guy. He just hated this man totally.

And yet maybe there was some change; maybe Crane had salivated the lean hard man. Maybe Crane had won. Maybe Gallery was lying dead: Wild gunshots could hit anyone by chance. So he might have to deal with the smooth Crane again.

There just wasn't any room for hesitation because he hated both men with the same gutsy desire to see them lying dead. Crane, the bastard, had tried to do him out of the gold. Gallery had figured to hand him over to the law. They were lousy double-dealing ginks – both of them!

Max Kerle crept up to the shack, expectant, wary as a wolf. He saw the two horses at the tie-rail and noted one thing instantly. The gold pokes were still tied to the saddlehorn of the big animal. And only some yards away was the horse that Gallery had used, standing with a tired droop to its head.

Max Kerle used his cunning brains, thinking

with swift animal deliberation. There was a rifle in the saddle-scabbard of Gallery's horse. Well, he needed that. And there was the gold, all there for the taking. Hell, things couldn't be better! But for how long? The situation might change. It would change. But a real hard-case like himself should never give up or give a sucker a chance.

And yet the need to know who had survived the shots was so strong in his evil mind, it was like a craving. Was Gallery alive? Maybe Crane was dead.

Life would be better when both were dead!

Max Kerle slowly withdrew the rifle from the saddle-holster and quietly checked the action. Pressing his ear close to the thick walls of the shack, he could hear some muffled talk. He imagined one voice was that of a girl, but the other could be any man. Was it Gallery or Crane?

Max Kerle waited outside the door, the rifle levelled, a leer on his sweat-grimed visage. His killer instinct was still strong. He would kill some guy!

He figured he would wait. The man inside the shack would emerge sooner or later. He'd walk into the night and into a shot from a rifle that would blast him into a pain-wracked heap – if not instant death. It was easy and he just had to wait. And not miss with a death-dealing slug.

He could not be sure if there was talk or activity going on inside the cabin or not. The walls were thick logs, hand-hacked by some unknown who had thought the spot was ideal for some use.

Max Kerle waited, hate swirling into his throat like bile. He would blast the first man who walked out of that door. Would it be Gallery or Crane?

Then there was a footstep – and another –

crunching into dirt, and the sounds were right behind him, something he had not foreseen. They just did not come from the doorway.

It seemed impossible. He hadn't figured on playing it this way. He whirled. Max Kerle saw for a nightmarish moment the menacing shape of the man with the Irish cut of visage – the man he hated.

Gallery! Right behind him – blast him!

He levelled the rifle swiftly. He had allowed it to momentarily sag. But the gun did not explode. The death-dealing flame did not spew from the gun. Max Kerle had allowed surprise to get the better of him.

An angry boot kicked out like a hammer from hell. Kerle's rifle was rammed up and backwards. The man had to make a frantic attempt to retain his grip on the weapon, and while he was struggling to do that, Jim Gallery bundled into him, sheer anger urging him to lay hands on the man rather than resort to a handgun.

It was maybe a mistake, but he wanted to send at least one man back to justice. Kerle would die for his murderous crimes – on a hangman's rope!

There was some satisfaction in ramming fists at the man's ugly face, feeling the knuckles thud into the damned flesh and feeling the hot spurt of the other man's blood.

Then a quick twist disposed of the rifle and it was flung to one side. Then they were slugging bunched fists at each other again, two men filled with a savage need to beat each other to pulp.

Jim Gallery could have ended the whole thing right there by just whipping out his Colt and firing into Max Kerle. Instead, he had this deep-down gutsy desire to hammer physically at the other man. And another fact – he wanted to take him back to legal justice.

But it was a mistake. Kerle seemed possessed by a vicious new need to survive, like his opponent. Weaponless, he fought and kicked. His hands clawed momentarily at Jim Gallery's face; digging in a few fearful moments at Jim's very eyeball sockets. Jim rammed him back and the fingers scraped down his face, taking blood and skin.

Sucking for breath, the two men backed from each other for about ten seconds.

'I knew you were there, Kerle,' Jim panted. 'I have this sixth sense – and I heard a click – a metallic click. It was you, Kerle, trying the rifle action. It was a good thing for me there was a loose plank on the other side of this cabin and I got out.'

Kerle's reply was a kick that nearly broke Jim's right leg. The man's boot connected so swiftly and with such damnable pain. The mistake in talking, in not killing this man, began to show.

Jim's leg buckled. He stumbled to one side. Kerle hit him again, a real thump that would have dazed even a prizefighter. Jim Gallery teetered, gasping, trying to gain time, sure that he could still best this man and take him prisoner.

At that moment Delia Breen chose to open the shack door and move into the night. Fast as a rattler striking back, Max Kerle saw his chance. He stepped back and grabbed at the girl, a real fast move. He held her like a shield before him. In his grim brutal grip, the slight girl did not stand a chance of escape.

Max Kerle had seen the Colt in Jim's holster leather; had figured correctly – he thought – that it was only a matter of time before the physical struggle ended with a gun blasting at him. The girl was his only chance, he thought. She was a hostage.

He backed away, dragging the screaming girl with him. In that moment Jim Gallery whipped out his handgun. Then he hesitated, cursing his luck. This turn of events wasn't to his liking.

'Let her go, damn you, Kerle!'

'You can go to hell, Gallery!'

Every passing second was another yard of getaway for Max Kerle. He knew the big horse that had belonged to Stephen Crane was right there behind him, and that was the animal with the pokes of gold. Sure, he was weaponless, but if he could only get away, beat the threat of the other man's gun, he had a chance.

Twice Jim Gallery aimed the Colt and trembled on the point of firing, but every moment was one in which the girl and her captor jerked and twisted. It was impossible to shoot without the risk of hitting the girl.

Max Kerle reached the big horse, laughed jeeringly, the girl still a living shield. He knew he had a problem. He wasn't away as yet. He still had to hit the saddle.

Out of a lifetime of dirty rough-house tricks came the answer. Gallery had a gun; he had the girl. Gallery, like the gent he was, would not risk her death. And death could come to this girl if he wished it because he knew how to kill her before the very eyes of the man with the gun.

Jim Gallery shook with fury and inner reproaches for having fooled with this ruffian. He had yielded to other considerations. They were rapidly looking like mistakes: unless Kerle made an error and offered a chunk of his anatomy as a target. But a moving man and a struggling girl made accurate shooting impossible. The Colt .45 was a handy if somewhat hefty weapon but it had limitations.

But the hard-case was close to the horse – the animal with the pokes of gold still tied to the saddle-pommel, Jim noted – and the girl was kicking and struggling in his sinewy grip. Kerle slid a hefty arm around her neck, cutting off her screams, almost choking her. And then Kerle played his ruthless card.

'Listen, Gallery – drop your gun. Yeah – bastard – drop it! Because if you don't I'm gonna break the neck of this little beaut right before your eyes.'

'You're bluffing ...'

'Try me! One jerk an' her neck is broken ...'

'I'd get you with a slug in the guts.'

'But she'd be dead, damn yuh! Are you going to chance that?'

Max Kerle knew darned well Jim Gallery was not in the business of playing fool games with a girl's life. The way he held the girl proved it was no idle threat.

Kerle had learned every rough-house trick in the book, among human garbage like himself. His arm was around the girl's throat so tightly that Delia Breen's breathing was becoming an ugly rasping sound. The man could choke her or break her neck.

Jim Gallery swallowed rage and disappointment like bad medicine but he still held his gun. His instinct was to level it at the moving man. But every moment the girl was in the way.

'I mean it, Gallery!' Kerle raged. 'I'll break her neck, so help me! You want that?'

The Killer Stamp

'I'd kill you!'

'The girl would be cold meat! I ask you again — do you want that?'

Jim saw the horror in the girl's eyes as her neck was forced back, slowly, cruelly, by the ruthless arm that held her. Seconds passed, her life in danger, with only moments to go. Shocked, Jim realized Kerle had bested him.

Jim Gallery's gun dropped to the ground. The night air eddied coldly around them, strangely chilling, as if to remind him he had been beaten. 'Let her go — now!'

Still mentally alert as any savage Indian, Max Kerle knew all his next actions would have to be thrust into seconds of swift movement. One thing — an implacable gun wasn't pointing at him.

He pushed the girl from him like a sack thrown from a train and with the same impetus he leaped to the saddle of the big horse. Kerle could move like a lithe animal when his hellish instincts reacted.

Hitting the saddle leather, he dug heels at the animal's flanks with complete cruelty. The horse, trembling with its own sense of danger, did not need spurs to rowel it. Nostrils flaring, the horse had heard the harsh bandied words between the two men. As Kerle thudded to the saddle, the mount sprang forward with coiled haunches.

Jim Gallery was, of necessity, moments behind all this play, and although he dived like a madman for his Colt again, there was only a disappearing shape in the night when he straightened on his feet and pumped off some desperate shots.

The gun spat flame and noise and slugs into the night air, but the whole circle of movement was too fast for accuracy. Chancy shots found only thin air, as usual. And with the luck of his breed, Max Kerle flattened on the saddle and tore into the darkness.

The girl sprawled motionless. Jim cursed. He hated to feel he had been bested. But Kerle was away into the night, seconds counting in the man's favour. Kerle had won. For the moment, damn him!

The girl looked in a bad way. He couldn't go off on the other horse in pursuit of Kerle while the girl gasped for breath.

He crouched over her and brought her round to some normality by gently patting her cheeks. A hard man, fists flying one moment, a death-dealing gun the next, he could still be kind when circumstances called for it. He saw her flutter her eyelids. Her eyes met his, a trifle fearful.

'You'll be all right,' he said. 'He's gone – damn him!'

'Please get me away from here. That hateful shack – and that dead man – I just want to get away.'

'We'll be ridin' out.' He nodded. 'We've got mounts. We'll get back to town.' He stared again at the silent dark land beyond them. There was something mocking about the way the night had helped Kerle, as if darkness and a villain were companions. The man was out there, covering distance, the rough land, and no doubt gloating.

'I'll get you into town and safety,' muttered Jim Gallery. 'And then …'

He did not finish his thoughts but he knew with a sense of grim finality what his next action would be. He'd go after Max Kerle. He would some day kill the man. He would retrieve the gold, not because of its value but because that was, and had to be, the end result.

The Killer Stamp

He had horses to round up and one body to tie over a saddle. He found Max Kerle's mount out in the night after some searching and making sympathetic noises to the crittur. He needed the animal for Stephen Crane's body. The big gent would travel back to town the undignified way – slung over a saddle, belly downwards. Was it a fitting end for a gentleman? Well, it was good enough for a human rat!

There were so many things to do. There was the journey back and a visit to Helen Mackay and explanations, and a call on the deputy in Delta. That galoot could have the body. He felt tired of it all but still grimly determined never to give up. Only the thought of meeting Helen cheered him.

When they were ready to go, the girl glanced back at the old shack. 'Hateful! How can I ever forget that awful man!'

'You will,' mumbled Jim Gallery. 'You're just a kid, Delia. You'll forget Crane.'

They rode back down the trail, bound for Delta, a horse on a lead rope and a cadaver over the saddle. They were tired, silent and moody. The girl was thinking about her dead father; Jim Gallery's brain brooding with thoughts of revenge. But they needed rest, bed and food. When they finally rode into Delta the night was silent and the saloons deserted except for those so dead drunk they sprawled where they were. Honest citizens had retired for the night.

Jim had to arouse Helen Mackay at her friend's home. Her reaction was womanly: 'You're in a terrible mess! Look at you! Blood and dust all over your face! Oh, Jim – you can't go on!'

'I've got to go after Kerle. He's got your gold ...'

She gasped. 'At this time of night! Oh, no! Look at the physical state you're in! Give it up. I don't care about the gold. It doesn't matter.'

'It sure does – to me,' he muttered. 'And being bested matters.'

'He'll kill you!'

'He tried. He was lucky. He got away – with that durned gold!'

Her brown eyes swept over him. 'You look terribly tired …'

'Thanks!'

'You need rest and food. Who do you think you are – some super-being? You can't ride all night and day. You'll fall off that darned horse with fatigue.'

Grinning faintly at her slightly bossy tone, he allowed himself to be taken in hand. He needed food – that was true. He needed some attention to the gouged cuts on his face. And he knew in his heart that Max Kerle would not ride all night because he, too, would need rest. The damned man would hole up somewhere. He'd have to be trailed and that would need time.

The deputy gave him a bunk in one of the cells, with extra blankets to show that this was preferential treatment, and he listened closely to Jim's story about Stephen Crane.

'He's a wanted man, as you'll find if you start checking on the truth. He and his pals in gunplay killed the sheriff. That's enough to indict him – but there's plenty more.'

The deputy nodded, narrowed eyes resting suspiciously on Jim Gallery's battered face and dirty clothing. 'And you, mister? You don't talk a lot about yourself. Who are you? Where'd you come from?'

'Just passing by. You need to know no more than that for right now. We can go into details some time when I've rested my bones.'

The man shut up, wisely deciding to make inquiries later. Jim finished his grub and rolled up in his blankets. He slept because he was bone-tired and with a head full of madly swirling thoughts that finally blacked out. But it wasn't the best kind of sleep.

He was up when the first light filtered into the cell. Walking stiffly, he went to a mirror. He figured to clean up, eat again and start to look like a human being that might impress a girl. With a grin, he tried the cell door. OK – the deputy had not turned the key on him!

He needed a fresh horse. He was going after Max Kerle and nobody was going to stop him.

Helen Mackay guessed he was itching to push on and trail Kerle, and she left her friend's house very early and intercepted Jim Gallery as he adjusted the cinch on a horse outside the sheriff's office. She noted his cleaned-up face – but thought his clothes were still a mess. She saw the gun in his holster. She also noted with some fear the rifle he had borrowed from the deputy.

'Jim, we don't need that gold ...'

'You and your father worked damned hard to win it,' he grunted. She saw that glint in his eyes; the determination behind it. 'Why should a louse like Kerle grab it? You asking me to back down – accept that situation?'

'You want to kill him,' she accused.

'He bested me. He might even come a-gunnin' for me again some day. There's things you don't know ...'

Yeah, Harry Carslake who still rode high and wide with the loot from the Drago Cattlemen's Bank.

She stared at him, worry and affection in her eyes. 'But killing, more killing, Jim?'

'Do you think I can rest when all I see in the back of my mind is that sneering devil?' There was almost rage in his question. 'No, Helen, I gotta go after him.'

About Harry Carslake, he wasn't sure. Would he hunt him down also? That had been the original driving force behind all his trail-riding. The man had the profits and he had killed and double-crossed in order to get it. Was it worth chasing? Looking for Carslake meant going back to the killer trail. It meant identifying himself with guns and death. Would he do that? Or should he turn to Helen and call it a day when Max Kerle came to a messy end with slugs tearing him apart?

Of course, this killing game could go two ways.

He said nothing to the girl about these thoughts. Anyway, he was unresolved about Harry Carslake, but Kerle and the gold would be tracked. Then maybe he'd think about Harry Carslake again.

Helen glanced again at the saddle scabbard and the Colt heavy in his holster. 'Guns! I always seem to see you with guns!'

Something made him take her arm tenderly. 'I can live without them ...'

'Will you try?'

'I'll be back, Helen – and you'll see. Now I'm goin'. That deputy seems mighty anxious to keep track of me. I'm ridin' out before he figures to come along with me. Adios, Helen ...'

He rode fast out of Delta, the horse fresh and

The Killer Stamp

frisky, forelegs digging easily at the soft earth. The watery sun was on his back. The day would heat up, he allowed. The grassy slopes just out of town still held the morning dew. But even with moisture in the air, dust kicked up beneath the flying hoofs.

Miles out, near a spread, he saw cowpokes chasing some cattle and, momentarily, he envied their settled existence. Now if he had ever owned land things might have been different.

He had a pretty shrewd idea where Max Kerle could head. Gold was something that most men like Kerle would want to turn into cash at the first chance, and they liked to spend – and that meant the amenities of a town. Crane, Dawson and Kerle could have done that in Delta but the opportunity had gone and now two were dead. So it was a pretty good guess that Max Kerle would head for Salida.

Jim Gallery drew an imaginary line in his brain, from the old mission where Crane had died to the direction of Salida, and he figured he'd reach that line after an hour or so of fast riding. After that he'd push on to the town, but hell only knew when or where he'd cut Kerle's trail again. Maybe he'd simply find the hellion drinking in town, drunk as a Mex and with the cash stashed away somewhere.

Maybe. There was always a maybe, something he didn't like.

As he rode, urging the willing horse on, he got the fixation in mind like a burr sticking to his vest; he'd get the gold back for Helen and her pa. That was the only reason for hell-trailing Kerle like this! And if the galoot got killed, that was tough luck!

But his whole line of thinking got a severe jolt when his horse went swiftly up a ridge and, poised, he found himself staring into a small valley.

There was a horse, lying dead, an ugly shape on the yellowed grass and shale. The colour of the animal's hide jogged his memory. This was the crittur Kerle had taken. Dead? What had happened? Where was the hard-case, Max Kerle?

Then, staring, eyes focussed ahead, he saw the small neat house only half a mile away, at the end of the grassy valley. Smoke curled from a stone chimney stack. Someone was there.

Thirteen

Jim Gallery crouched over the dead horse. He noted at once that the unfortunate animal had broken a leg. And someone had put a slug into the big head. Wal, that had happened some time ago because he had not heard the echoes of any shot. And it was unlike Kerle to spare a horse's misery.

That brought him up sharply, thinking. He remembered that Max Kerle had been gunless when he had ridden out into the night. The man had lost his rifle when it had been wrested from his grasp. And he had no handgun. But someone had shot this cayuse.

There was no doubt that this was the horse that Max Kerle had used to get away from the old shack near the mission. And the saddle and other gear was missing. Naturally, there was no sign of the gold.

Once again Jim Gallery stared at the little clapboard and stone house in the distance. On further examination, he knew the place belonged to some homesteader; the tended land and garden plots around the building were evidence of hard work by some person. He suddenly heard some hens cackling; the sound of some milking cows in a barn. The smoke from the chimney signified people. Was Max Kerle there? Or had he stolen another horse and taken off?

Jim vaulted to his saddle again and went on, his hat pulled down over his eyes. When he got really close and could discern the clean, chintz drapes at the small windows, the door opened and a girl stepped out.

She held a shotgun in her two hands, her face pale and sternly set. She pointed the gun at Jim Gallery and he drew in his cayuse.

'This is as far as you go, mister. What do you want?'

His lips twisted in a quizzical smile and he drawled: 'Just passing, ma'am. I mean no harm. Tell me, have you seen that dead horse out there?'

'I have. Why – why – do you ask?'

'You'll get the buzzards.' Jim smiled, taking some time, staring at the shotgun and seeing a great deal more. The girl was young, her straw-coloured hair twisted into a bun at the back of her head and she wore a cheap gingham dress. He noticed the plain wedding ring on her finger and he wondered where her husband was right now. She was an attractive young woman, lithe-bodied and with some freckles. As he stared, drawing out the time, he noticed her apprehension. He was sure he wasn't the cause of this fear. So he smiled back.

'Broke a leg,' he said casually. 'Did you shoot the crittur?'

She hesitated. 'Er – yes – yes –'

'One of your horses, is it?'

'Yes. Go away. Ride on, mister. We've had trouble – with – drifters – before –'

'I ain't that kind of drifter. Leastways, not the troublesome sort. Hmm – one of your nags, huh?'

'Yes ...'

'How come it broke a leg?'

'Please ride on – go –'

'Or you'll use that scattergun, huh?' Jim smiled again. 'You got some water nearby, ma'am?'

'There's a well at the back of the house ...'

Jim nodded, wheeled his mount and walked it around the gable-end of the homestead. He saw the well and went to it and cranked up the bucket. He let the horse drink and he slopped some water over his own face. All this casual activity took up some time and he became more than sure the girl was not alone. It was just a hunch and to a galoot like himself hunches were important.

She had gone inside the house when he rode around to the front again. He rode the horse out to a rocky bluff where the valley turned and that was the limit of his retreat. He sat hunched in the saddle and pondered. He was pretty sure the girl had been forced out to make a show with the scattergun.

Kerle. It was a fact that the dead horse had been his mount. The girl had lied about that. And quite likely she had not shot the beast. But she could have made a gun available to Max Kerle. Under some compulsion? Where was her husband?

Jim Gallery had a feeling of grim certainty that he need ride no further in his sombre search for Max Kerle. The man had holed up in that homestead. His reasons were not so obvious. A picture of the slender, pretty girl came to him again and with it a hunch that women – like gold – were a lure to evil men.

He would play a waiting game, but what was happening inside that outwardly peaceful house?

He didn't intend to wait until it was dark in order to learn the truth.

The house fronted mainly on to the wide valley, but behind the place he had noticed the rising mounds of yellow dirt, the gullies and broken areas of land. That was the best way to approach the house. If he went back across the valley, they'd see him for a mile.

He edged the horse out of the hiding-place; went right down the valley, knowing he could not be seen behind the rocks, and then returned through a number of gullies barely high enough to hide him. Soon he was behind the homestead, as near as he'd ever get and still stay in cover. He hitched the horse securely to a tough root that grew out of the earth in the side of the gully.

There was no hesitation, no hanging back. He had to go on, discover if his theories were sound, and the best way was the fast way.

There was open ground between him and the house; a kind of grassy waste which was yellowed with too much sun. He had to cross it. He knew he could be seen. But if he went as fast as an Indian approaching a target, he might succeed.

He leaped forward, feet as silent as possible and, crouching went ahead in a swift race to the side of the house. It was a good hundred yards' sprint and he made it without inviting a gunshot or any other sign that he had been seen. He waited, drawing quick breaths. He listened, searching for a clue as to the occupants of the place. He had seen the girl. But who else was there? He figured the damnable Kerle might be there. But was that all?

And then, as if a signal to his probing mind, a shrill scream came from inside the house. This

The Killer Stamp   151

must be the girl! Then he heard a torrent of sobs and protests.

'No! No! Leave me alone. Oh, no – please!'

His face harsh, Jim raced to the door, darting along the blank gable-end. Hunches based on a number of sticky situations in the past told him that this was the time to burst in, when some uncontrollable activity was going on.

Gun in hand, he rammed against the main door to the house and found it was not locked. He went in like some minor tornado and halted when he found himself in a big living-room.

And right there he froze!

'Hold it, Gallery!' Max Kerle's order rapped out.

There was every reason to obey.

'You can drop that damned hogleg for a start!' Kerle's second order followed instantly.

Jim Gallery took it all in like a flash. Kerle was holding the girl easily, although she was a strong creature, and he was also pointing a gun menacingly at the head of a man lying on a couch.

'You don't give up,' snarled the gangling hawk-like man. 'I'm sick to hell of you, Gallery. Drop that gun – or I'll blast this feller's brains out on that couch!'

It was another rotten set up that seemed to be a special trick of Kerle's. Jim nearly triggered in sheer desperation, finger itching to get a result, but every warning nerve in his head told him he could easily kill or wound the girl. Max Kerle held her, just as he had held Delia Breen the other night. The girl did not keep still. She was jerking and twisting in panic and fright, which was understandable. Her dress was torn and pale skin showed. Once again Kerle was using dirty tricks to best a man!

'I'll kill this galoot if you fool around any more, Gallery!' The warning was savage, thick with hate and murderous intent. Jim knew Kerle could kill in cold blood. A hot slug and death to a man was Kerle's answer to most situations.

Jim Gallery dropped his Colt. He saw it hit the wooden floor with a kind of bitterness that nearly choked him.

'Better!' sneered the other man. 'Now ain't this cosy? We might be able to relax – until I get organized.'

'Don't count on it, you louse!'

'Heh! Heh! Now I take it you got a cayuse somewhere …'

Jim Gallery ignored the remark. 'What's wrong with him?' He pointed to the man on the couch.

'Gut-trouble!' sneered Kerle.

'He's my husband.' The girl glanced imploringly at Jim. 'He's ill – some sort of fever – I don't know what. I've been nursing him …'

'Pretty little nurse, ain't she?' Kerle held her in a strong insolent manner, his hand close to a breast. 'I've been hangin' around hoping she'll be nice to me – but it seems I got to take everything I want in this life!'

'Let her go, man. I've dropped my gun.'

'You kiddin'? Ain't she pretty? And all alone – at least she was until you showed up, Gallery. You're always just behind me, ain't yuh? The hell with you, Gallery. I'll kill you!'

'You lost your horse?' Jim figured to ask questions; play for time.

'Broke a damn leg, the stupid nag …'

'You shot it? You should have dragged the carcass away somewhere and I'd never have noticed it and probably would have ridden by.'

'Does that matter now?'

Max Kerle looked the epitome of evil intent. His face was ugly, with untidy beard and whiskers. His hair was wild. His clothes were torn and filthy, the results of fights and hard riding. In fact, the man looked hardly human, with lines of anger and evil stamped into his face. Dried blood and bruises still lay on his face. Jim wondered fleetingly if this was the final image for any man on the owl-hoot trail. Was it possible for any man to become such a stringy, smelling scarecrow?

Kerle jerked his gun. 'Move over, Gallery. Get away from that Colt. Hell, I could plug you right now. Ain't that somethin'? I got you dead to rights, Gallery, damn your guts!'

'You got me,' said Jim placatingly. Inwardly, he thought: *You are filth, man! Your carcass will live with the devil and rot!*

'You still got the gold, then?' Jim wanted to rile the man, although that was risky with a guy who was bordering on madness.

Kerle indulged in a raucous laugh. 'Stashed right here – in this house. I got all the aces.' Some need for satisfaction stalled Kerle's finger on the trigger. He eyed Jim Gallery as he held the girl masterfully in spite of her continuing struggle.

'You've got the aces,' agreed Jim.

'And a girl – Heh! Heh! A man always needs a gal.'

There was a curiosity, a sort of speculation in Max Kerle's glittering eyes, showing that he knew Jim was at his mercy. 'You'll die here, Gallery – you know that. I just got to squeeze this blamed trigger. Durned funny, ain't it? I mean, you and me, all we done together, with the blasted sarcastic Crane hombre deader than rotting carrion – an' Kid Dawson dead meat – just leaves me in one piece after all that hellin' around.'

'I'm in one piece, too,' said Jim Gallery.

He watched the girl jerk again and wondered how long Kerle could hold her. And how long would the man's talking spasm last?

'You've tried to kill me.' Anger began to edge into Kerle's voice. 'More'n once. So it's right for you to die, Gallery. Wish to hell I could make it a slow death. Ever seen a man pegged out with a hot fire burnin' into his chest? That's Injun-style. Pity I can't hand it out to you.'

The young wife began a fresh burst of resistance. A new fury drove her on, it seemed. Max Kerle spent a full two minutes just beating down her strength with an arm that was like a band of steel. The gun in his right hand never wavered from the body of his enemy.

'You will pay for this in the end, my pretty,' Kerle grated a warning. 'I'm goin' to have you. Been a long time since I been with a gal as fresh as you. You'll come to me – unless you want that sick husband of yourn to get his come-uppance. Surely you'll do that for your man!' And Kerle laughed at his sick joke.

She became strangely silent, as if with a new thought. She even lay back in Kerle's cruel grip, her breasts rising and falling with her exertions. She glanced at Jim Gallery as he stood tautly, his hands upraised enough to placate Kerle. Then she looked into the unlovely visage of Max Kerle. Eyes wide with fear, she seemed to arrive at an awful decision.

'I'll come with you – now – if you promise to leave my man alone. Promise not to harm him – please –'

Kerle's laugh was thick with triumph. 'Wow! I'll treat you right, my beauty! Max will show you –'

'His promises are pure evil,' Jim warned. 'You could trust a desert rattler more ...'

'You shaddap, Gallery – or I'll plug you right now!'

She slid from his arm as his grip slackened slightly. He fastened on to her hand until the knuckles showed white. She paused, looked at him. 'You'll leave my man alone – please –'

'Sure. Sure.' An ugly sound escaped Kerle's throat. 'By hell, you're all woman, my pretty. And you, Gallery – you're dead!'

'Let him go,' breathed the girl. 'Let him ride away ...'

Max Kerle levelled his Colt. 'Not a chance. I hate his guts.'

'You just can't kill like that!'

'He's bested me – tried to kill me. I tell you – he's goin' to die! Heh! Heh!'

The girl was still attempting to drag her hand from Kerle's vicious grip. She was moving to a door on the other side of the room which might be sleeping quarters. Jim Gallery watched, scowling grimly at his helplessness. Had he a chance to jump Kerle? Could he beat a Colt which would be triggered fast? But Kerle kept at a distance, although he moved a few slow edging steps with the girl as his hostage.

The man on the couch gave a sudden moan and writhed as some fever wracked him.

'My man – he's ill! Show some mercy – leave.'

'I'll blast Gallery first.'

'I don't want killing in this house,' cried the girl. 'It's been a lovely home – so happy – but you wouldn't understand.'

Her hand was still gripped by the dirty paw of the villain and he moved with the girl. Then with a taunting smile which only gave Kerle's face an uglier appearance, he halted.

'I'll blast this damned nuisance in my life,' he snarled. 'Then we'll spend some time together, my pretty. You won't regret it. I reckon I need a woman – and I'll not touch a hair of your goddamn hubby's head.'

Max Kerle half-turned and began to level his gun with the appearance of finality. The girl was at least two steps away from him, her eyes fear-filled and on the unkempt man. Kerle had released her hand.

Jim Gallery knew the end was pretty nigh to hand. If he hesitated another second or two, a slug might tear into his flesh and that would be the end of Jim Gallery. No more trails to ride ... dead man ... and Helen a million miles away and in another dimension.

He thought Kerle would not err in this final, vicious accurate shot! The man knew the hogleg in his hand!

Knowing it was a desperate try, that he was a guy gambling with his own life, and knowing there was nothing else left in the book of tricks, he dived for Kerle's feet with all the crashing speed he could summon from his body. His breath rasped into a hoarse cry as he shot like a jet for the filth-encrusted boots. Even as he shot like some projectile, despair filled him, knowing that he had no chance to beat a slug travelling faster than any human being could achieve. He'd die. A shot would crash out at any split second and rip the life out of him.

He touched the man's feet, clawed, hoping to unbalance him.

Then the shot roared out in the close confines of the homestead living-room. A yell of agony seared the homely room and echoed like the dying howl of some ungodldy animal.

The yell did not rasp out from Jim Gallery's throat.

Jim Gallery rolled, fast wits telling him in a shattered moment that something had happened; that he had a chance to live. Someone else was going to die!

He tumbled like an acrobat across the floor, almost frenzied. He turned on his hands and knees to glance at the scene.

The girl had a gun in her hand and smoke still wisped from the barrel, the acrid fumes slowly eddying. Jim recognized the weapon. His gun, the one he had dropped at Kerle's command! The girl had picked it up, very fast and triggered with swift young hands.

As for Max Kerle, he was on his knees, his face twisting in pain, his eyes glaring in horror at approaching death. Blood already stained a patch on his shirt, oozing swiftly and horribly as his heart pumped with the last muscular spasms. Blood mixed with the dirt on his shirt that seemed to be the hellion's trademark. His gun fell from his fist as his head sank and he emitted harsh gurgling sounds. Then he fell face forward.

The young wife stared, slowly lowering the

handgun. Jim Gallery jumped to his feet; went over and gently took the instrument of death from her. She glanced at him, her face breaking into sudden tremulous movements as reaction flooded every nerve of her bring.

'I had to do it!' She breathed the statement. 'That animal – I wouldn't have given myself to him.'

'I know,' said Jim Gallery gently.

'I just figured – if only I could get that gun – so I had to play him along – so awful – but I fooled him, didn't I?'

Jim stared at Kerle on the floor, a lifeless hulk that dripped blood and smelled unpleasantly of death. It didn't seem possible after all this time that the man was dead. He and the other two desperadoes, with their lust for gold and anything illicit, were boothill meat.

'You saved my life,' said Jim. 'And you rid the world of this hellion. I'm glad, in a way, because you saved me the job of pulling a trigger.'

The girl clutched at a chair and sat down. She tried to pull her torn dress together. 'Who was he? Not that it matters – he's dead – isn't he?'

'Ready for the mortuary. And don't worry about him. He was just one of the killer stamp –'

'He – he – came here early this morning, full of some plausible tale, and borrowed a gun to kill the horse. Then he started to show his awful intentions the moment he returned to this house. I stalled him for a long time – pleaded with him – he seemed to enjoy making me squirm.'

'That was his style, my dear …'

'And then you rode up. He forced me to go out with the shotgun. I was terribly scared –'

'You don't need to tell me any more.' Jim

holstered his gun. 'I'll help you clean up, get this skunk outa your house. He's goin' back to Delta and boothill. And I'll see a doctor about your husband.'

Jim found the gold. The girl showed him where Kerle had stashed it. He sat down and looked at the small pokes of the heavy metal for a long time, hard lines etching his face at his multitude of thoughts.

There was still Harry Carslake, one man who rode free and laughed at him; a man who relied on a fast horse and guns to keep all the advantages of the loot from the Drago Cattlemen's Bank.

Jim Gallery hauled Kerle's body on to the hard-baked ground outside the homestead. He went back and helped the girl clean up as he had promised. He watched her at one time as she bent over her husband, wiping his face with a damp cloth. At that moment he thought of Helen Mackay.

'I'll get my horse an' then I'll go, ma'am,' he said. 'And once again – thanks for saving my life.'

'You saved me by just turning up.'

He grinned and waved. As he rode down the valley, the unlovely body tied to the back of his saddle, he thought again of Harry Carslake. There was only one answer; the hell with him! He had had enough of the vengeance trail. Let Carslake ride on and on forever, and spend the rest of his life looking back for a pursuer.

In Delta, he found Helen again. She was talking to the deputy in the sheriff's office and, at a glance, she ran to Jim the moment she saw him. She hugged this tall grim-faced man in the travel-stained range gear.

'Oh – you're safe – thank goodness!'

The deputy eyed the body on the horse, staring through the window. 'Another cadaver?'

'A killer who's quit killing.'

'I'll get him to the mortuary,' sighed the lawman. 'You can tell me the yarn – but I think I know enough.'

'Good – because I want to talk to this lady.' He took Helen to a quiet corner out on the boardwalk and placed an arm around her shoulders. 'It's all over. I mean the shootin'. There'll be no more if I can help it. And I want to tell you all about myself ...'

She searched his face, smiling shyly. 'I think I know enough about you, Mister Jim Gallery – but tell me as much as you want if it will do you any good.'

'It will ...'

'One thing I know – you're a real man. You fight for justice.'

He nodded with some finality. 'Guns and justice – oh, let's forget all that stuff. I'm cleaning up an' taking you to some nice place where a man and a gal can eat and talk – about the future. That's important – our future.'